BLUE AUTUMN CRUISE

For Jeff, Etta, and the Pearson family

We want to hear from you. Please send your comments about this book to us in care of zreview@zondervan.com. Thank you.

ZONDERKIDZ

Blue Autumn Cruise

Copyright © 2012 by Lisa Williams Kline

This title is also available as a Zondervan ebook.

Visit www.zondervan.com/ebooks

Requests for information should be addressed to:
Zonderkidz, 5300 Patterson Ave. SE, Grand Rapids, Michigan 49530

ISBN: 978-0-310-72617-3

Cover design: Kris Nelson
Interior design: Sarah Molegraaf
Editor: Kim Childress

Printed in the United States of America

12 13 14 15 16 17 18 19 20 /DCI/ 18 17 16 15 14 13 12 11 10 9 8 7 6 5 4 3 2 1

SISTERS IN ALL SEASONS

BOOK THREE

BLUE AUTUMN CRUISE

BY LISA WILLIAMS KLINE

ZONDER**kidz**

ZONDERVAN.com/
AUTHORTRACKER
follow your favorite authors

Acknowledgments

Special thanks to Frederic J. Burton, director of the Blue Iguana Recovery Programme, for patiently answering my questions about blue iguana hatchlings. His book *The Little Blue Book, A Short History of the Grand Cayman Blue Iguana*, is a fascinating account of the heroic efforts of a large group of volunteers to save this rare and ancient creature from extinction. He captured my imagination with personality profiles of many of the iguanas that have been rescued by BIRP. Since my book is fiction, I have taken certain liberties with iguana behavior, and any inaccuracies are strictly my responsibility.

Another thank you goes out to my dear writer friend Chris Woodworth for reading yet another manuscript of mine and making such creative and helpful suggestions. Thanks, too, to my critique partner Liz Hatley for her comments and support. Ann Campanella and her daughter Sydney always make such sensitive observations and their gentle suggestions inspire new scenes and angles. When Sydney wrote me that while reading my books she sometimes forgets to eat, it was a compliment of the highest order.

Thanks to my dear friend Betsy Thorpe and her resourceful daughter Georgia for answering my questions about life with type 1 diabetes, and for reading and commenting on the scenes dealing with it. I admire Georgia so much, who is cool and level-headed and lives a happy, healthy life with diabetes.

My walking partner, Deb Waldron, deserves great credit for listening to me endlessly ruminate out loud over plot twists.

This series of books would never exist without Caryn and Kim. Thanks to Jennifer Lonas for her thorough proofreading; I really felt like she had my back! Thanks also to the staff at Zondervan for designing such beautiful books for the series.

And last but not least, I'd like to thank Etta Kline, my mother-in-law, for making it possible for me to write about going on a cruise! Our family cruise for her 85th birthday was an unforgettable experience.

1

DIANA

A curling line of taxis glinted in the Florida sun, snaking across the huge parking lot, inching forward, and cutting each other off. Horns blew and people yelled.

I leaned out of the back window of our taxi, gasping at the size of the cruise ship at the end of the parking lot. The ship loomed like a painted iceberg, its sparkling white sides rising up and up into the sky. Suddenly it sounded its horn, which was booming and deep and lasted several seconds.

"That's our boat, girls!" Mom said, pointing. "Isn't it beautiful?"

The boat looked like a tall floating island. On the top deck, tiny people leaned against the railings. Some of them waved.

"Will you look at that thing," said Norm, my stepdad, who was sitting in the front passenger seat. He gave a low whistle. He'd tried really hard to be good to me, but it had been tough adjusting to Mom being married to Norm. It used to be just me and her against the world.

"Oh my gosh!" said my stepsister, Stephanie, as she leaned out of her side of the taxi. "It's ginormous! How many floors does it have?"

"I think they're called decks, honey," Norm said.

"How many decks, then?" She started counting, got messed up at about eleven, and started again.

The taxi behind us blew its horn. We lurched forward.

Mom, Norm, Stephanie, and I had flown down to Fort Lauderdale, and we were meeting other members of the family on the ship. It was Stephanie's grandmother's seventy-fifth birthday, and Grammy Verra wanted everyone to help her celebrate, so she invited the whole family to come with her on a birthday cruise to Grand Cayman, an island in the Caribbean. Grand Cayman was famous for its reefs and its snorkeling and scuba diving. Mom said it was also famous for its conservation of endangered species of animals.

I had only met Grammy Angela Verra once before, and that was at Mom and Norm's wedding April before last. She was slim with short silver hair, and she'd worn a silver, sparkly top to match. "So I have a new granddaughter," she'd said to me at the reception, placing one hand on each of my cheeks. Her voice sounded young, not an old-lady voice at all.

"Not your real granddaughter," I'd said, stepping away.

"Real enough for me," she'd said. "And I think it's just great."

Then for my birthday in August, she'd sent me a musical card that played "Celebrate Good Times" when you opened it. Whenever she called she insisted on talking to everyone in the family, including me. "Tell me what you've been up to," she'd demand. She took yoga classes, and she had a dog named Botticelli, or Jelly for short. She'd been nice so far, but I basically didn't trust people.

I would see what happened.

On the cruise, besides Grammy Verra, I would meet

Norm's sister, Aunt Carol, her husband, Uncle Ted, and their two kids. Their family hadn't been able to come to the wedding. Lauren was fourteen, Stephanie's age, a year younger than me, and Luke was ten. Stephanie had known these cousins her whole life.

At first I figured they could knock themselves out having a great time on the cruise and leave me out of it. When everyone first started talking about coming on the cruise, I said I'd go stay with Dad. But Mom never even asked him.

"We're a family now, and we do things as a family," Norm had said. "And that's how it is." He was big into us being a family these days.

So, here I was, not knowing anyone. Zooming around about an eight on the Moronic Mood-o-Meter. Dr. Shrink had given me this lame rating system for my moods, one to ten. One being in the depths. Ten being zooming all over the place. I'm supposed to try to stay at about five. She said that this trip would be a challenging time for me, blah, blah, blah. No kidding. A whole new family. Everybody was probably thinking I was a trouble maker. And with Stephanie practically like a sister to Aunt Carol's kids.

And I missed the barn. I missed Commanche, my buddy, the horse I rode most at the barn. He didn't ask me questions about my moods. He just came to the stall door to greet me and twitched his ears when I talked to him.

When Mom and Norm first got married, I lived with them and Stephanie lived with her mom and only came to stay with us every other weekend. Mom and Norm always acted like it was a special occasion when she was here, making plans for movies and stuff. Since we started high school this year, though, Stephanie had been living with us full time. I think she asked to. Something about her wild stepbrother, Matt. So instead of bringing her overnight bag and staying in the guest room, she had dragged over tons of mostly pink stuff and turned the guest room into a pink palace.

When we first got to know each other, on a summer trip to a mountain ranch before eighth grade, I started out being mean to her. I made fun of her clothes, her fancy jeans, and pink boots. I even made her horse spook. We were so different. She was prissy and afraid of everything. But she helped me free the wolves. We got into a lot of trouble together. Last spring at our trip to the Outer Banks, we got in trouble again, but Stephanie had been cool to me. She defended me. I started feeling more like I could trust her. I started feeling that maybe we could be a family.

But Stephanie moving in with us had changed things.

It had changed the whole way the family worked. I actually liked it more, and I didn't think I would.

I glanced over at her, beside the other window, wearing the hot-pink skort and top she had been jokingly calling her "cruise wear." I just wore my regular jean shorts. Mom had brought home some white shorts with a bunch of tops for me, and I'd said, "No way." But we were going to have to dress up one night during the cruise. Mom made me try on the bridesmaid's dress I wore to their wedding, but over the past year and a half, I had grown, and it was too short and tight, so she'd gone out with Stephanie and bought me a new one. It was purplish with some ruffles on the front that Mom and Stephanie both insisted were in style. Ruffles! I was dreading having to wear it. And I couldn't stand the fact that they bought it for me together.

Now Stephanie was up on her knees trying to count the upper decks. She was excited about seeing her cousins. They'd probably be fake nice to me. I bet they'd talk about me behind my back. Talk about how I had mood problems and had to take pills.

Now the cab driver turned to Norm.

"I can't get any closer. You'll have to get out here and walk."

"Okeydokey," Norm said, and he slapped his hand on the back of the seat. "Let's do it, folks."

And so in the middle of the parking lot, with all the engines idling and the waves of heat rising around us, we piled out of the taxi and grabbed our luggage. Mom had made sure my new suitcase had wheels, so I pulled it along behind me as we wove through the maze of cars. Stephanie's suitcase was bigger than mine, and she had to wedge it sideways between two taxis. It fell over. Typical.

As usual, I went over and helped her.

"Oh, thanks, I'm just too excited or something," Stephanie chattered as I flipped her suitcase upright and got it settled back on its wheels. "Aren't you excited?"

"Sure," I said.

"We're rooming with Lauren," she added over her shoulder as we walked single file between two yellow taxis. "She's great. You'll love her. This is going to be so awesome!"

"Yeah." I'd seen pictures of Lauren. You could tell she and Stephanie were cousins; there was a definite family resemblance. She had dark hair, like Stephanie, and her olive skin was the same too. But she was taller and more athletic-looking. She played soccer and volleyball, I think. And in every picture I'd seen, she was laughing.

Was I going to "love" her the way Stephanie said? How many people in the world did I love, anyway?

We got closer and closer to the ship and were soon walking in its enormous shadow. I craned my neck to look up, up at the decks rising above me. A slanted walkway led inside the ship. Mom carried our tickets and passports, so she went first.

We had to leave our luggage in a big warehouse-looking room. The cabin stewards would bring our suitcases to our staterooms later. We got our room numbers and headed into the ship, ending up on a landing with wide flights of stairs and elevators with golden doors and fancy patterns in the maroon carpet. On either side of the stairways were long, thin corridors with rows of closed doors. Other passengers, looking as confused as I felt, stood beside the diagram of the interior of the ship and tried to decide which way to go. Crew members in neat, short-sleeved white shirts hurried by, their feet skimming the stairs.

"Okay, this is our deck," Mom said. "I think our rooms are closer to the back of the ship, so I think we should turn left and go down this hallway."

"Shouldn't we turn right and go that way?" Norm said, pointing to the diagram on the wall.

I was completely turned around. I didn't know where the front of the boat was, or where the back was. I didn't know which direction was the land and which was the sea.

"This way, I think," said Stephanie, heading into the narrow corridor, then turning left. After staring at the diagram of the ship for a few more seconds, we all started following Stephanie and watching the room numbers as they went up.

"Great, Stephanie, you've always had a good sense of direction," Norm said.

I looked at Stephanie's back ahead of me, and I thought I saw her straighten her shoulders. Such a daddy's girl.

We followed the straight, narrow corridor all the way along the side of the ship until finally we arrived at our rooms.

"Look!" said Stephanie. "Our names!"

She pointed to a card beside the door frame with fancy printed type: Stephanie Verra, Lauren Whitt, and Diana Williams.

Mom gave us both our key cards. Her and Norm's room was right next door to ours. Just as I slid my key card through the card holder, the door flew open from the inside.

"Hey!" the girl inside squealed. It had to be Lauren. Long dark hair and olive skin like Stephanie. She was taller than Stephanie though, with a more athletic build, and with a longer, slimmer face.

"Lauren!" Stephanie squealed at the same time.

I was right in between the two of them, and they jumped in front of me so fast to hug each other, I had to duck to get out of the way.

"Oh my gosh, you look so cute! It's so great to see you!" Lauren cried.

"You too!" said Stephanie.

"Hey, Lauren!" said Norm, giving Lauren a hug. "This is my wife, Lynn, and her daughter, Diana."

Lauren stepped back from hugging Norm and looked at Mom for a second, and then hugged her too. "Hi!" she said. "It's so exciting that you guys got married. I wish I could've come to the wedding."

"We do too," Mom said.

"Hi, Diana," Lauren said to me, politely wrapping her arms around my shoulders too. "It's great that we're going to have a chance to get to know each other on the cruise. Stephanie's told me a bunch about you."

"Probably complaining about me," I said.

Mom and Stephanie both gave me a look. Oops. I should have stopped to think about that one for a few extra seconds.

"No," said Stephanie slowly. "I wasn't."

"Of course she wasn't, Diana," Mom said, pointing to her temple with the signal Dr. Shrink had given us to show when I needed to stop and think about what I was saying and doing.

"Whatever," I said, looking at the floor.

"Well, we're going to have a great time," Stephanie said quickly.

"Yes, yes, yes!" Lauren said, jumping up and down. "They have ice-cream sundaes right now on the pool deck—let's all go."

I shrugged. "Okay."

"Daddy, can we go get ice-cream sundaes now?"

"Well—"

"Attention, passengers!" a disembodied voice with a foreign accent broadcast through the corridor. "In thirty minutes' time, all passengers must report with their life jackets to their muster stations. Repeat, all passengers please report with life jackets to their muster stations in thirty minutes' time."

"Muster stations? What's that?" Lauren asked.

"The place you're assigned to go if there is any emergency," Norm said. "We should stay together for that, and then maybe you all can go get sundaes afterward. Where are your parents, Lauren?"

"They're right next door—that way." She pointed. "My brother is staying in the room with them. Grammy gets a special room since it's her birthday—she's on a higher deck, and she has a balcony."

"Lucky Grammy!" said Norm.

"We need to write down everybody's room numbers so we can get them straight," Mom said.

"I want to see our room!" Stephanie said. Lauren stepped back to let Stephanie in, and I followed her.

The room was tiny. Across from the door, a wall featured a round porthole the size of a beach ball. Through it you could see part of a lifeboat, and beyond that, the ocean and sky. Against the wall next to the door, and also across from it, were two sets of narrow bunk beds. A tiny desk with drawers was attached to the fourth wall. Two small, U-shaped easy chairs were arranged around a small circular table, and behind it a small refrigerator was set into the wall. Everything fitted together perfectly.

"Everything's so tiny and cute!" Stephanie said.

A Lilliputian-sized bathroom lay behind a small latching door, with a tiny sink, commode, and shower. Trial-sized bottles of shampoo and conditioner and a selection of soaps and lotions were artfully arranged around washcloths and hand towels that had been folded to look like monkeys.

"Look at the monkeys!" I said to Stephanie and Lauren.

"That is so cool," Stephanie said. "Can you believe the three of us are going to be staying in our own room together like this? I am so excited!"

"I know!" Lauren said. She took Stephanie's hands, and they jumped around the room squealing. Spare me.

"I took this bottom bunk," Lauren said, sliding onto the bunk and crossing her legs, with one flip-flop dangling.

"Do you want top or bottom, Diana?" Stephanie said with a quick look at me.

I glanced at Lauren. She probably wanted Stephanie to take the other bottom bunk so they could lie in their beds and talk to each other.

"I don't care," I said. "I'll take the top." I knew they weren't trying to leave me out. They had tried to include me. They were just happy to see each other. Still, I wished there was a barn somewhere I could escape to.

2

STEPHANIE

I could hardly believe we were going on a cruise! And Lauren and I were going to get to be together for five whole days. I swear my hands were shaking, I was so excited. Grammy was the best grandma ever.

I knew Lauren and I had to be very careful to include Diana, and don't think I hadn't been thinking for weeks about how to do it. It was going to be weird. I mean, Lauren and I had been close practically since we were born. Anyway, we were not going to leave her out, but I knew Diana, and she might just leave herself out. If she did, I hoped Daddy and Lynn would understand.

Lauren sat down on her bunk, and so when Diana said she didn't care what bunk she got, I took the other lower bunk. I had always been a little afraid of high bunks, anyway.

"So, Steph, are you cheering again this year?" Lauren asked.

"Yeah. What about you, are you playing volleyball or soccer this fall?"

"Soccer. I'm mid." Lauren pulled her dark hair into a ponytail, then let it fall back on her shoulders. "I'm awesome, I'm just sayin' ..."

"Modest too!" I poked her and laughed. Lauren was always like that.

"Yeah. Keeps me out of trouble. Hey, they have so much going on that I want to check out," Lauren said, picking up one of the daily schedules that had been left on our desk. "We get to go to a show every night if we want to. They also have a thing you can sign up for where they take you back into the kitchens. We can watch them making three hundred key lime pies or whatever. And they demonstrate how to fold the towels like animals. And they have a scavenger hunt and a *Harry Potter* trivia contest. We should play!"

"Ooh, yeah, I want to," I said. Lauren had always been the kind of person who liked to be doing something. She didn't like to sit around and talk that much. In that way, she was like Diana. I worried about whether they would get along. Diana had a hard time getting along with people, period, and sometimes Lauren was bossy.

"Check this out," Lauren said. She held up a small flip video camera. "I'm going to videotape people while we're here."

"Who are you going to videotape?" Diana asked. She'd chosen the bunk above my bed and was lying there with her cheek propped on her elbow. She'd been in a hurry this morning before catching our plane, so she'd barely ripped a comb through her flyaway, strawberry-blonde hair. She had that kind of hard, intense expression on her face that she got when she didn't really understand why someone was doing something. Since I'd gotten to know her, though, I'd figured out that she wasn't being judgmental; she was just puzzled.

"Anybody and everybody!" said Lauren, holding the camera in her lap. "It's going to be, like, my oeuvre during the cruise. It will be my trademark. Everyone will know me as the video girl."

"Some people won't want to be videotaped," Diana said. "Like me. It makes me nervous."

Lauren picked up the camera and aimed it at her. "Really?" She gave her voice a reporter's tone. "So … what about being videotaped bothers you?"

"Lauren!" I said with a light laugh.

"I was just kidding around," Lauren said, putting down the camera.

Diana didn't say anything about Lauren's joke. She just had a scowl on her face.

"But seriously, you should get used to being video-taped because we have to document our trip," Lauren said. "Right now we should go wander around the ship and find out where things are."

Just then there was a knock on our door, and when we said "Come in," a dark-haired, handsome man in a short-sleeved, white uniform pushed the door open. He had broad cheekbones and coffee-colored skin. "Hello and welcome," he said. "I am Manuel, your cabin steward. Is everything all right so far?" When he smiled at us, he had really even white teeth.

"When do we get our luggage?" asked Lauren.

"We are working on it," said Manuel. "The young ladies need to be patient! In a few moments you will need to go to your muster station. It is important that everyone go."

"That's like if we're the Titanic," said Lauren.

"Don't even say that!" I said. I noticed that Manuel

was holding a key ring with a photo of children on it. "Are those your children?" I asked.

Manuel held the photo up. "Oh, yes, they are! That's my family. If there is anything you need, please don't be afraid to ask," he said, and then he ducked out the door.

A minute later there was another knock on our door, and Aunt Carol, Uncle Ted, and Lauren's brother, Luke poked their heads in.

"Hey, there, Stephanie!" My aunt and uncle both came in, and I jumped up and gave them each a big hug. Aunt Carol smelled like perfume. Uncle Ted smelled like a cigar. Luke, who is ten, with reddish hair, and small for his age, acts like a miniature little old man. He is the most serious boy ever.

"Hello," he said, holding out his hand for us to shake.

"And, hey, Diana, we just met your mom. We're so glad to get to meet you finally. Welcome to the family!" said Aunt Carol.

Diana sat up on her bunk, keeping her head low so she wouldn't hit the ceiling, and swung her legs back and forth. "Nice to meet you."

"Has Lauren already interviewed you two on video?" said Uncle Ted. He was a big man with a cheerful, booming voice, and he was wearing a striped golf shirt and khaki shorts. "She's obsessed with that camera. You have to try to get out of the way."

"Dad! I'm going to document our trip!"

"You need to be careful you're not documenting people who don't want to be documented," said Uncle Ted.

"Dad, chill," said Lauren.

"I don't want to be documented," said Luke.

"You never know about people," said Aunt Carol. She had Daddy's same brown eyes and wavy, dark hair. Like Mama, she wore lots of jewelry. She and Mama were still good friends, and sometimes they emailed each other. I wondered how Aunt Carol would get along with Lynn. I was always wondering about whether people were going to get along. Maybe I worried about that too much.

An announcement boomed over the loudspeaker system: "Attention, the general emergency alarm is about to be sounded. Repeat, the general emergency alarm is about to be sounded. This is the alarm you would hear in case of a real emergency, and you would be required to report with your life jackets to the muster station."

Then the ship's horn sounded seven short beeps and one long beep. The beeps were so loud and deep they kept reverberating inside my head.

"Attention, you have just heard the general emergency alarm. Please proceed with your life jackets to your assigned muster station."

Aunt Carol held up her bulky, orange life jacket. "Okay, everybody, let's go."

Diana slid down from her bunk, and the three of us girls reached into the top of the closet and pulled down our life jackets.

"Are they going to tell us how to put these on?" Diana asked. "It's pretty obvious." She put her arms through the armholes, then started arranging the belt around her waist.

Lauren put the back of the life jacket on top of her head and let the armholes hang down over her ears. "Like this, right?" She started laughing.

"No, you dork," I said, laughing too.

"Come on, girls. Let's not be silly," said Aunt Carol.

"Yeah. Straighten up," said Luke.

Just then Daddy and Lynn poked their heads in. "Let's see who can figure out where the muster station is," said Daddy.

We studied the map on the back of our door, and in a minute or so, Lauren and I were racing down the long hall toward the elevator and stairway landings. Luke was right behind us.

"We go down one floor!" Lauren yelled, and she skidded into a landing, ready to race down the steps. Luke pulled in front of me and started to race past us.

"Hold it, hold it!" said a staff person standing guard

at the landing. "We should be orderly and walk while going to the muster station, not race."

"Oops, sorry," I said, trying to slow down.

"Sorry!" said Lauren in a voice that didn't sound sorry at all. And Luke kept on going.

I checked behind to see if Diana was still there. She was plodding along with her hands resting on top of her life jacket belt and a mad look on her face.

"Hurry up!" I said as I followed Lauren and Luke down the stairs.

When we got to the muster station, more of the crew members were there, and people were standing around with their life jackets on. After waiting for everyone to get there, one of the crew demonstrated how to put on the life jackets. Lauren was giggling, and one of the crew members had to tell her to be quiet and listen. Then everyone put on their life jackets. Daddy and Lynn came over to make sure Diana and I had them on right, and then the crew members came around.

While the crew members were counting us and going over the evacuation routes, Daddy put one arm over my shoulder and the other around Lynn. I don't think he meant to leave Diana out; I guess he only had two arms! And probably she wouldn't have wanted his arm around her, anyway.

I watched Diana standing off by herself, and for some

reason I felt guilty. I remembered a time my friend Colleen was over at the house and we asked Diana to play cards with us, and Diana was really rude when she said no. Then I told Colleen that Diana liked animals better than she liked people. Colleen had laughed. But then only a few days later, some kids started calling Diana "annn-i-mal" in the hall at school. When we switched to the high school this year, I hoped that people would forget all about it, but they were still calling her "annn-i-mal." It really hurt her that people called her that, and I hadn't been able to get up the courage to admit to her that it was because of something I said.

I was brought back to the present by one of the crew members, who was announcing that the muster-station meeting was over. As soon as we put our life jackets back in the room, Lauren went next door and asked her dad if we could go to the pool area and get an ice-cream sundae.

"We're going to be leaving port shortly, and it'll be fun to stand on one of the upper decks and watch," said Uncle Ted, poking his head around the door to our cabin. "Let's all go together. This is a big ship, and we wouldn't want to get lost. "

"They can't make us stay with them the whole time," Lauren whispered to me.

"I don't want to get lost," I whispered back. Then I

noticed that Diana was watching us whisper to each other with a jealous look on her face. As soon as Uncle Ted stepped out of our room, I caught her eye.

"Lauren is just frustrated that our parents want us to stay with them the whole time. She wants us to be on our own."

Diana looked thoughtful, as if she was considering whether I was really telling the truth, and then she nodded. She trusted me. That made me feel even worse when I thought about the "annn-i-mal" thing.

Pretty soon all of us were on the elevator on our way to the upper deck to watch the ship take off. Exploring the ship was amazing. Once we got off the elevator on the top level, we walked out onto the pool deck. People were already sitting around the pool in their bathing suits, and four boys a little younger than us were in the pool playing.

"Marco!" shouted one.

"Polo!" shouted the other three.

"It" lunged after the voice that was closest, and the others swam away, sending spirals of water soaring. We dodged away with little screams.

"Look at that giant movie screen!" Lauren said, pointing up behind the pool. The movie screen was literally as tall as a two-story house. As we were climbing up onto a deck that looked down on the pool, the ship sounded its horn again.

"Ooh, we must be leaving!" Lynn said. I suddenly noticed the deep vibration of the ship below my feet, which must have been caused by the ship's engines, but I couldn't remember when it had started. We ran and stood against the railing and looked down on the tiny people and vehicles below us as the ship slid out of its berth. People began to wave and yell "Bon voyage!" and we waved back. My heart was beating wildly, the sun sparkled over the water, and ship flags flapped in a stiff breeze. We began to slide by the other cruise ships that were docked in Port Everglades. Then we passed by the tall buildings of Fort Lauderdale lining the beach. A wave created by the wake from our ship rolled across the water and broke on the sand.

Then just behind us, we heard Grammy Verra's voice. "There you are!"

We turned around, and there was Grammy Verra, in her white cruise wear, a bright purple shirt, and sunglasses. "I was afraid I'd never find you on this big ship!"

"Grammy!" I threw myself into her solid arms, and she pulled me close.

"Look at you, sweetie!"

Next she hugged Lauren. "What kind of trouble have you been getting into lately, missy?" she said with a laugh.

"No trouble, Grammy, I promise," Lauren said, slanting her eyes at me and laughing.

Then Grammy hugged everyone else. Diana hung back, but Grammy said, "Come over here now, I'm going to hug you too!" She kept exclaiming how wonderful everyone looked and how excited she was about the trip. "I am just so glad we were able to all get together for this," she said. I had always thought that Grammy's voice sounded like music.

"This is going to be one heck of a birthday for you, Mom," said Daddy.

"You bet!" said Grammy, laughing. "Diana," she added, "are you ready for this?"

"I'm not sure," Diana said, kind of looking at her feet.

"It's a lot of family members to meet all at once, isn't it?" Grammy patted Diana's arm. "You'll be just fine, I know it. We'll all have a great time. And I have the three most beautiful granddaughters on the ship, that's for sure."

I always felt like beaming when Grammy complimented me. I liked the way she was including Diana. I hoped Diana was appreciative of how hard everyone was working to make her feel included.

"You'll have to come see my room," Grammy said. "I have a balcony. If anyone wants to come sit on my balcony, you're welcome to anytime."

"I want to!" I said. I had always liked talking with Grammy about my life. She always had good advice. I wanted to talk to her about how things were working out with me now that I was living with Daddy, Lynn, and Diana. I knew I would miss Mama, and I did … a lot. But I loved Lynn; she had been so nice to me. Diana and I fought a lot at first. I hated fighting with people, and sometimes Diana just picked fights for the fun of it. But I had to get away from Matt, my step-brother who flunked out of college. He was so mean to me. And now Daddy, Lynn, Diana, and I were trying to feel like a family.

A few days ago, on a Tuesday night, Daddy and Lynn called a family meeting after dinner. We hadn't ever had a family meeting before, and I didn't know what to expect. Diana and I finished up the dishes, and then we both came into the family room slowly. Daddy and Lynn were waiting on the couch, and Diana flopped onto the easy chair, propping her riding boots on the coffee table with a big annoyed sigh.

"Diana, no feet on the coffee table, please," Lynn said.

Diana clomped them on the floor.

"We wanted to have a talk with you girls, now that we're all living together, about being a family," Daddy said, taking Lynn's hand. "I really want us to feel the love and loyalty for each other that a family feels. I know it's hard to get used to a new family unit. I have something I'd like us to do together that might help, and that's start going to church."

"No!" said Diana. "I'm not going."

"Wait a minute," Daddy said. "Last spring Stephanie and I went to church at Eastertime, and it really brought home to me how much God means to me and how much I missed church. We hadn't really gone since before the divorce. Well, now we're making a new start, and Stephanie and I have gone a few more times, and now Lynn says she's willing to go too. I'd like us all to go."

"Mom?" Diana said accusingly. "You said that?"

Lynn nodded her head, putting her other hand on top of Daddy's. "I did. I know you and I haven't gone to church, Diana. But I want us to be a family, and I agree with Norm that one thing that might help us bond is going to church together. I'm willing to try it."

"I'm not going to make anyone go," Daddy said. "You girls are old enough to make your own decisions. But Lynn and I are going to go, and we hope you'll decide to go with us."

"I'll go," I said. I liked church. It was comforting to me to think that there was a God out there who loved me.

"Not me," said Diana. "Is this family meeting over?"

She held up her fingers and did air quotes to frame "family meeting."

I had had a sinking feeling then. When we got back home, we'd be going to church and having to leave Diana behind. I wanted to talk to Grammy about what that would be like.

"I'd love for you to come visit and see my balcony, Stephanie," Grammy said now.

"Great!" I said.

"Look how small and faraway Fort Lauderdale looks already!" Aunt Carol said, leaning on the railing.

And it was true. Lauren had her camera up to her eye now, first focusing on Fort Lauderdale receding into the distance, and then turning the camera on me. I love being on camera.

"Grammy's birthday cruise has officially started!" I said, throwing my hands above my head. And then I turned a cartwheel right there on deck.

"Yippee!"

3

DIANA

I wished Lauren would quit sticking that camera in everybody's face. I felt like throwing it in the ocean. How was I going to get along with her for five whole days? And Stephanie obviously thought she hung the moon.

The next thing Lauren did was make us all go over to the station where they were serving the ice-cream sundaes. None of the grown-ups wanted one, except Norm, but all of us kids got one. Some smiling crew members served them up, and Mom didn't even say anything about saving room for dinner later. Stephanie loves posing for the camera, so Lauren shot video of her clowning around while she was eating her sundae. Lauren had this annoying habit of acting like a TV narrator when she was taking the video. Luke had a thing where every time Lauren pointed the camera at him, he'd freeze stock-still.

"Luke!" she said the second time he froze with his spoon halfway to his mouth. He stayed frozen, with ice cream starting to drip. I thought it was a pretty good idea and thought maybe I'd try it. That would teach her to try and videotape me. So far she hadn't.

"Come on," Norm said as soon as we finished. "Let's find out where things are on this ship."

The tour was confusing. There were three elevators on the ship, and seven restaurants, nine bars, three swimming pools, a work-out facility, a casino, and a spa, where we were sending Grammy for her birthday spa day. A whole hall was dedicated to displaying pictures that were going to be taken on the trip. Trying to keep track of what was in the front of the boat ("Forward," according to Uncle Ted) and what was in the middle (amidships) and what was in the rear (aft) wasn't easy.

After that, Grammy got tired of walking and said she was going back to her stateroom. Stephanie gave

Grammy a hug, as she headed for the elevator. "I'll meet you guys at dinner," Grammy said.

Norm still wanted to find the putt-putt golf course, so we walked to the back of the ship and then took the elevator up to the very top floor. We stepped out of the elevator into a small room where you could pick out any putter and any color ball you wanted for a round of free putt-putt. Opening the door to the outside, we stepped into high winds whistling around our ears. Surrounding us was the putt-putt golf course, covered with this green flannel material, and a basketball court enclosed in netting, with a running track encircling them. We decided not to play, but it was amazing to stand on the track and look back over the shining ocean and the boat's wake at Fort Lauderdale, now a dot in the distance.

"What a view," said Norm. "Can you believe we just left there?" He pointed to the tiny skyscrapers of Fort Lauderdale on the edge of the horizon.

Birds flew alongside us. Some were pelicans. Some were seagulls. I couldn't believe I was going to be away from animals for five days. No barn. No horses. No Commanche. I felt a stab of homesickness. I thought about the way he stuck his head over the stall door when I came to the barn in the afternoons. He'd probably wonder where I was.

Since I was on the cross-country team last year, I decided to run around the tiny track a few times. It was so small I'd probably get dizzy going around it! Still, running was something I liked to do when people were getting on my nerves—like Lauren with her video camera—and I thought I might come here again.

When everybody was heading back to the room to get ready to go to dinner, I lagged behind. I let Stephanie and Lauren walk along, nearly arm in arm, giggling together. Once Stephanie looked back and said, "Come walk with us, Diana," but I just told her to go ahead. Mom noticed that I was walking alone toward the back of the group, and she waited for me, then walked along with me as we went back by the swimming pool.

"So, what do you think? This boat is amazing, huh? We're going to have a fantastic time, aren't we? And I thought Grammy was really sweet to you." She tried to put her arm around me as we walked, but I stepped away. Hanging around with my mom was the last thing I wanted to do when I was feeling left out.

"You know, Stephanie and Lauren have a lot of memories together. Sometimes you'll feel left out since you weren't there. Just try to remember they're enjoying being together, and they're not leaving you out on purpose, okay?"

Did Mom think I was a moron? Finally Mom got the message and went ahead to walk with Norm. I watched him put his arm around her and speak reassuringly to her. I knew I'd hurt her feelings, and he was trying to make her feel better.

Then Stephanie came back to talk to me. "Hey, Lauren and I are going to make a 'day in the life of a cruise' video. We want you and Luke to help us."

"I don't like the video camera," I said. My voice sounds so much higher on the video than it does in my head.

"You don't have to be in it. You can run the camera if you want. We just thought it would be fun to do something together."

The 'rents were probably making them include me.

"What's Luke going to do?" I said

"I don't know. We haven't figured that out yet." Stephanie touched my arm, and I looked into her brown eyes as she made an appeal. "C'mon, Diana. I want us all to get to know each other and have fun. Lauren is so much fun if you give her a chance. Will you?"

I walked along a few strides with Stephanie, thinking about how things had been different since she'd moved in with us. I didn't have to share my room with her, and since she had cheerleading practice every day, she wasn't home until dinnertime. But when she was home, she was always having friends over. I never felt like I had Mom to myself. Once I came back from the barn—Josie, the barn manager, had given me a ride home—and Mom, Norm, and Stephanie were sitting in the family room laughing and joking around. It seemed like everyone stopped laughing the minute I walked into the room. Like they all had a great time except when I was around.

But at other times, Stephanie had been nice to me. Whenever she had a friend over, she'd invite me to join them, even though most of the time I wasn't interested. She sometimes had this girl, Colleen, over. But I didn't trust her. Stephanie did try to help me with my English homework, though. And whenever she went downstairs to get a cookie, she'd always bring one up for me. That was the thing; she was always nice. Sometimes I wished she'd just lose it and act horrible. It was just so hard to believe that anyone could be that nice all the time.

"Well," I said slowly. "I'll try. But if it gets on my nerves, I'm going to quit."

"Fantastic! You'll try it!" She grabbed my arm and squeezed. "It's going to be so fun." She went back and joined Lauren again.

We passed the buffet and then rode down the elevator and went single file down the long hallway back to our rooms.

"We'll head over to the restaurant for dinner in about thirty minutes," Norm said as he and Lynn went into their room. "We'll come to the room and get you."

"How about we meet you over at the restaurant?" Lauren said. "We can find our way!" I could tell she was dying to be on her own on the ship.

"No, not just yet," said Aunt Carol. "The first time we go to this restaurant, we'll all go together. Once we learn our way around the ship a little bit, we'll give you kids more freedom. Don't forget, girls, you have to look nice for dinner. Tonight isn't dress-up night, but no short shorts or anything like that."

"Okay," Stephanie said. "See you in a few."

I was the last one to walk into our room.

"It's driving me crazy," Lauren was saying. "I feel like I have an umbilical cord attached or something. Like we're little babies. I wish they'd just chill and let us be on our own more."

"Well, it is a really big boat," Stephanie said. "I think you need to chill. I don't mind being with the 'rents at first, until we learn our way around better."

"I want to go see where the crew stays. I saw some online videos of cruise-ship crews, and they have their own mess hall and their own bar and everything. I want to take my video camera down there."

"I can't wait till dress-up night," Stephanie said,

looking at herself in the full-length mirror beside the door. "What does your dress look like, Lauren?"

"I brought two. One's short and blue and off one shoulder. Dad said I look at least seventeen in it," Lauren said.

"Big deal," I said. "Why do you want to look older?"

"I just do," Lauren said, giving me a funny look. "Why not?"

"Diana's on the cross-country team at our school," Stephanie said, suddenly changing the subject. "She's really good. So you guys are both good runners. Maybe you could run on the track together while we're on the boat."

"That track was so teeny," Lauren said.

"I know. I ran around it a couple of times, but I was afraid I'd get dizzy," I said, laughing.

"I know, right?"

"But you guys could still run together one day," Stephanie insisted.

"Sure, maybe," I said noncommittally. If I went up there to run, it would be to get away from Lauren, not be with her. I climbed up on my bunk and lay on my elbow, looking down. This sure was a little room.

"Anybody want me to French-braid their hair for dinner?" Stephanie asked.

"Oh, me!" said Lauren.

I lay on my bunk and watched as Lauren settled on the bunk in front of Stephanie, and then Stephanie separated Lauren's shiny dark hair into sections and started to braid it.

One time at home, Stephanie had talked me into letting her braid my hair. She'd come in my room and sat on my bed, and I had to admit it had felt good for her to smooth and comb my hair. At dinner that night, Mom and Norm had complimented me on how nice it looked.

"That would be a good way to wear your hair when you ride," Stephanie had said when I checked out myself in the mirror. "It will fit better under your riding helmet than a ponytail."

Now Stephanie and Lauren talked and laughed as Stephanie worked. I didn't want to watch them but I couldn't help myself.

"My dad has a new saying," Lauren said.

"Ha-ha, a new one?" Stephanie said. "What?"

"What he says all the time now is 'At the end of the day.' He picked it up from the news, I think. I just want to crack up. He says it about everything."

"What does it mean?" Stephanie said.

"I guess it means when all the evidence is evaluated, or when everything is all over. 'At the end of the day,'" she said in a reporter's voice, "we will all be paying higher prices. Now if he says it tonight, you can't laugh!"

"At the end of the day, I promise I won't laugh at your dad saying 'at the end of the day,'" said Stephanie, giggling.

"I hope that, at the end of the day, you won't," said Lauren.

"Remember last time we visited you guys, his saying was 'It is what it is'?"

Stephanie laughed. "Oh yeah, and we were at dinner at your house, and he said it about ten times, and we were, like, rolling in the floor. Every topic ..."

"It is what it is," Lauren said in a dadlike voice. "And before that it was, 'Been there, done that.' And before that it was 'I went ballistic.' He always picks up whatever sayings are cool or popular."

Stephanie giggled. I turned over. I told myself they had known each other their whole lives. I told myself they weren't trying to make me feel left out. I told myself they were just remembering stuff they'd done in the past. I told myself I didn't care.

"Okay, done!"

Stephanie straightened and smoothed the braid a few times. Lauren went over to the mirror on the wall and held up a hand mirror so she could see the back of her head.

"Oh, excellent, girl," Lauren said. "Thanks."

"Diana, you want me to do yours?" Stephanie said. "It looked so nice the time I did it at home."

I shouldn't have said yes, but I did. And so Stephanie braided my hair, and then Lauren braided Stephanie's, and we all had braided hair for going to dinner the first night. And of course Lauren wanted to videotape us. And I agreed. I don't know why I did it.

So Lauren videotaped Stephanie and me smiling at the camera and then turning our heads around so the camera could see the braids. And for some reason, we started singing this song on the video. It was called "The Lion Sleeps Tonight." It's an old song, but everybody knows the words. There is one part where you sing "In the jungle, the mighty jungle, the lion sleeps tonight," and then you sing, "Aweemaway, aweemaway, aweemaway, aweemaway," and it sounds really funny.

So first Stephanie went skipping across the room singing, "Aweemaway, aweemaway," and when she got to the side of the room I was on, we put our heads together and sang, "A-we-um-um-away."

And then Stephanie said, "You do it, Diana!" And so I did. I skipped across the room and back singing "Aweemaway, aweemaway," and then met up with her, and together we sang, "A-we-um-um-away." Lauren about dropped the camera, we were laughing so hard. I couldn't believe I did that. Stephanie made me do it.

And I was kind of having fun, I have to admit it.

4

STEPHANIE

Just as we finished singing our very ridiculous version of "The Lion Sleeps Tonight," Daddy knocked on our door and called us to come to dinner. I was so excited that the three of us were having fun together. And I felt like we all looked pretty and grown up with our braided hair. Even if we were singing "Aweemaway."

The restaurant was beautiful! Murals of Italy were painted on the walls, and four round white columns stood in the center of the room. Hanging from the ceiling were gorgeous chandeliers in gold and glass. The tables were covered with long white tablecloths and were set with sparkling glasses for water and wine, with a cream-colored napkin folded on each gold-rimmed dinner plate.

Grammy was the first one there. She had claimed a big round table for us and was sitting there all alone. "Finally! There you are! Over here!" She waved her arms energetically. "It's a good thing I got here early and got the table," she said.

We laughed as she gestured to the empty tables all around. When we sat down, two cute waiters came up, dressed in white, long-sleeved shirts and brocaded vests, with white aprons tightly tied around their waists, and they handed us heavy menus covered in leather.

"Good evening," said the first waiter, who was tall and pale with dark hair. "I am Bogdan, and I am from the Ukraine. I've been on the ship for eight months."

"And I am Luis," said the second waiter, who was shorter and stocky, with shiny dark hair. "I'm from Mexico, and I've been on the ship for five months."

"So you don't get to see your families for all that time?" Grammy asked.

"No, we stay with the ship. But we get to go to wonderful, exciting places," said Bogdan.

"What's the most fun place you've been?" Lauren asked as she held the video camera up and pressed the Record button.

"Rio de Janeiro," said Luis.

Bogdan scratched his chin. "I would say Barcelona, Spain."

Luis and Bogdan told us they would be our waiters every night for the whole five days, and that they would be back in a few minutes to take our orders.

I opened my menu and discovered that the names of the dishes were in Italian.

"Oh my gosh!" said Lauren. "I have no idea what any of these things are."

"What a great learning experience," said Uncle Ted. "No chicken tenders tonight!"

Although the names of the dishes were in Italian, the description of each dish was in English. There were several different courses, including *"antipasti,"* which were appetizers; *"zuppa e insalata,"* which was soup and salad; pasta; and the main dish.

When Bogdan and Luis came back to take our orders, we had a lot of questions for them. They allowed me to order ravioli as my main dish, even though it was listed under "pasta." Diana ordered stuffed chicken, which was called *petto di pollo*, and Lauren who said she was an adventurous eater, ordered lobster, which was called *aragosta*. Luke ordered spaghetti.

"Can I taste your lobster?" I asked Lauren.

"Sure!" she said.

Dinner went by in a blur. I focused on using my best manners. My ravioli melted in my mouth, and Lauren's lobster, when I tried it, had a rich, sweet taste.

"What are you girls going to do tomorrow? We're supposed to be at sea all day," said Grammy.

"Go swimming!" said Lauren. "And maybe play some basketball. I'd like to try out that court that's up there near the golf course."

"There's one pool where they play a lot of games, and then there's another where it's supposed to be quiet for adults," said Lynn. "And then there's a small pool at the very back of the ship."

"I've heard that you have to get out early to claim a lounge chair," said Daddy. "You girls shouldn't sleep too late. You'll miss getting a spot by the pool."

"They have a teen nightclub!" said Lauren. "Can we go tonight?"

"Sure," said Uncle Ted. "But the three of you will need to stay together."

"We can go by ourselves, right?" Lauren asked.

"We'll walk you up there just to see where it is," said Daddy.

"Come on, we can find it ourselves!" Lauren said.

"Be patient, Lauren," said Aunt Carol. "All in good time."

All during the meal, Luis and Bogdan paid special attention to us, even though the dining room filled up with people.

"The staff is so attentive," said Lynn. "Service is really a big part of the cruise experience, I can see."

"It must be a challenge to live on the ship for months at a time. Think how small the staff rooms must be," said Daddy.

"At the end of the day," said Uncle Ted, "I would say the service is the key to a vacation on a cruise ship."

He said it! Uncle Ted said "at the end of the day." I glanced at Lauren, and we pressed our lips together. I looked away from her to keep from laughing.

A minute later, I couldn't help it, and I looked back at her. She had put her hand over her mouth to cover up the laughing.

Before I could stop myself, I let out a giggle. Then Lauren did too. We looked away from each other quickly and tried to stop.

"Girls? What's so funny?" Aunt Carol said.

"Nothing," Lauren said. Then she burst out laughing.

I laughed too. Uncle Ted, when I looked at him, was concentrating on his steak. I cut my eyes over to Diana. She knew what was going on. She'd heard us talking about Uncle Ted's sayings.

"Okay, do you girls want to share the joke?" Daddy said. "The rest of us feel left out."

"Never mind," Lauren said. "It's nothing. Sorry."

"They're laughing at the way Uncle Ted says 'at the end of the day,'" Diana said quite loudly.

"What?" Uncle Ted looked up.

I felt my face go hot and my scalp start to prickle. I couldn't believe Diana had told! How could she do something like that? Now Lauren and I were so embarrassed.

"Oh," said Daddy, "you're making fun of your 'rents, huh?"

"We don't mean anything by it," I said all in a rush. "We just noticed that Uncle Ted has new sayings each time we see him. We were just teasing."

That was such a mean thing Diana had just done to us. She'd purposefully tried to make us look bad. Just because she was feeling left out. Which as far as I could see was her own fault. We'd been trying to include her the whole time. I'd been looking at my lap, but when I glanced up I saw Lauren looking at Diana with narrowed eyes.

"I'm sorry, Uncle Ted," I said, feeling so awful.

"Well, I tell you," said Uncle Ted suddenly. "Some people will go ballistic if you make fun of them. At the end of the day, I don't mind a little teasing."

All the grown-ups laughed, but Lauren was still giving Diana a dirty look. Diana's jaw was set and her expression was stony-looking.

"That was a good way to handle it, Ted," said Grammy Verra.

In a minute the grown-ups had started talking about something else. I heaved a sigh of relief. When we had finished dessert—chocolate mousse for all the kids, and tiramisu for the adults—Lauren wanted to go directly to the teen nightclub without going back to our rooms. Daddy said he'd walk us up there because he wanted to see where it was and what it was like. I was fine with that, but I could tell that Lauren was dying to go wander around the ship on our own. Diana said she didn't want to go.

"Oh, you should go," Lynn said to her. "Give it a try. If you really don't like it, you can come back to the room."

I watched Diana look at her lap. The way I was feeling right now, I didn't care whether she came or not!

We walked toward the front of the ship, rode the elevator up to one of the top floors, and found the teen nightclub, which was called Cabaret. The walls were bright blue, and there was a funky blue-and-yellow pattern in the carpet. Small round tables surrounded by chairs were positioned around the room. High stools attached to the floor surrounded a shiny metallic circular bar. Against one wall stood one of those giant, colorful jukeboxes with flashing lights.

On another wall was a huge video screen where underwater scenes were showing. In one corner of the room was a console where there were joysticks and video editing equipment.

It was early, only 8:30, and hardly any people were there. One of the staff members stood at the door wearing a black T-shirt and pants. He looked like he was in his twenties.

On one side of the room sat a group of girls who were definitely older than us, and they were laughing and making fun of the place. On the other side of the room stood boys who looked like they might be our age. One was skinny with very short dark hair that looked almost military. His clothes looked like his mother had ironed them. The other was less skinny and had a long shock of brown hair that he kept flipping off his forehead. They were both kind of cute, especially the one with the longer hair.

"Hey, I'm Josh," said the staff member at the door. "How old are you girls? This is the teen club, and it's for kids ages thirteen to seventeen."

"We're fourteen and fifteen, all freshmen in high school," Lauren said.

"This is the place for you, then!" He turned to Daddy. "We're just about to start a game."

"What kind of game?" Lauren asked. "I could get into a game!"

"We're going to play a getting-to-know-you game, and then later we're going to play karaoke," said Josh. "You can also shoot and edit videos. At the end of the cruise, we're going to broadcast some of the teen videos on the ship's TV channel."

"Ooh, really? I have my own video camera, but I don't have that many features on it," Lauren said. "Editing would be really cool."

"Well, you can try it out in a bit," said Josh.

Daddy and Uncle Ted waved good-bye to us. "We'll see you girls later," Daddy said. "Can you find your way back to your room?"

"Absolutely!" said Lauren excitedly.

"I think so," I said.

"We expect you back in your rooms by eleven. Check in with us when you get back. We hope you have a good time, at the end of the day!" said Uncle Ted.

Lauren laughed. "At the end of the day, we will!"

"Let's get started with this game!" Josh sat on the floor, and the three of us joined him. Slowly, the two boys came over. The older girls said they didn't want to play.

"No problem, that's cool," said Josh. "What we're going to do is you're each going to introduce yourself and tell us three things about yourself. Two of those things will be true. One of those things will not be true. We're going to try to guess which thing each person says is not true. I'll start. My name is Josh. I'm from California, and I played middle linebacker on my high-school football team."

We were all silent for a minute.

"You didn't play middle linebacker for the football team," said the skinny guy with the supershort military hair and neatly ironed clothes. "You're not big enough to play middle linebacker."

"Ding, ding, ding! That is correct!" said Josh. "Okay, next?"

"I'll go!" Lauren waved her hand. "My name is Stephanie Verra, and I'm fourteen and I love to flirt with boys."

I could feel my face turning hot. I felt like saying, "Lauren!" But I didn't say anything. Did Lauren really think that I loved to flirt with boys?

The two boys glanced at each other and laughed. "I believe that you love to flirt," said the one with the shock of brown hair falling on his forehead. He had a habit of tossing his head to the side to throw back his hair. "So I think that's true."

"So you think either her name or her age isn't true?" said Josh. "Hmm. What do you think?"

"I think you are fourteen. So Stephanie's not your real name," said the skinny guy to Lauren.

"Ding, ding. Correct!" said Lauren.

"So, what is your name?" Josh asked.

"Lauren. My cousin is the one whose name is Stephanie."

Diana was supposed to be next, but she said she didn't want to play.

"We'll come back to you later," said Josh. "Maybe you'll change your mind."

The skinny guy said his name was Evan, that he was fifteen, and that he had once been hit by lightning.

"You've never been hit by lightning," Lauren said, laughing. "You wouldn't be here."

"Or else I would have, like, smoke coming out of my ears or something. Anyway, you're correct," said Evan. He turned to his friend. "Okay, your turn, dude."

"My name is Guy," said the boy with brown hair. "I'm a diabetic, and I won the national science fair when I was in fourth grade."

"Hmm," I said to Guy. He was really cute. "I'm going to guess ... that you did not win the national science fair."

Guy gave a quick toss of his head to get his hair out of his eyes. "Right."

"So ... you're diabetic?"

Guy nodded. He showed us the small pump he used to deliver insulin. It was attached around his waist and looked like a little cell phone. A tiny line led from it to an injection site to the right of his belly button.

"You wear that all the time?" I asked.

"Yep," he said. "It delivers insulin continuously to my body."

At that point more kids came in, and Josh had to leave to greet them and talk to their parents. Then he started giving out glow-in-the-dark necklaces and turned up the music.

"In about ten minutes we'll start the karaoke!" he said.

The five of us sat in a circle for a few minutes, and then Lauren got up and went over to the video-editing booth. "I want to learn how to work this," she said.

"Me too," said Evan, following her.

Pretty soon Lauren had her video camera out.

I started talking to Guy about how he found out he had diabetes, and Diana sat there listening to us. While we were talking, Lauren must have figured out how to show the footage from her camera on the system in the club, because suddenly during a lull in the noise, on the big screen on the wall came up a video clip of Diana skipping around the room and singing "Aweemaway" at the top of her lungs. Everyone in the club burst out laughing, including the three older girls who hadn't wanted to play the game with us.

Lauren looked over at Diana with a look of triumph on her face. Diana's face turned completely white, and her mouth dropped open.

I couldn't believe Lauren had done that. But I knew she'd done it to get back at Diana for telling on us at dinner.

5

DIANA

Oh, I couldn't believe it! How could she have done that? Why did I let her tape me singing that song, anyway? That was so stupid.

I was so mad, I couldn't even stay at the club for another minute. I jumped to my feet, listening to all the laughter, then I ran out the door and jammed the elevator button with my thumb. Anything to get out of there in the fastest way possible.

Lauren was so mean! I wished we'd never come on

this cruise. I wished Mom had never married Norm. I wished I'd never met Stephanie.

Why couldn't we just go back to the way things were before? Before we'd gone to the Outer Banks last spring I'd thought if things got bad with Mom, I could just go live with Dad, but now I knew that really wasn't possible. Dad didn't want me to live with him. That was pretty obvious. But how could I stand things like this?

There were already kids at school who made fun of me. They would growl at me and call me "annn-i-MAL" when they walked by in the hall. Every time it happened, it was like someone stabbing me in the heart.

The elevator came, and I jumped in and hit the button to close the door. That minute I saw Stephanie and the boy named Guy running out of the club toward me. I hit the Close Door button about five more times, and the doors started to close.

But Stephanie raced across the lobby and stuck her hand between the doors just as they were closing. They started to open up again.

"Diana! Don't! I can't believe she did that. I'll talk to her! Don't leave, okay?"

"Leave me alone!" I said. "People make fun of me at school. And now they make fun of me in the middle of the ocean too! I am not staying here anymore, with everyone in there laughing their heads off at me."

"I didn't laugh," Stephanie said.

"I didn't laugh either," Guy said. "I make it a policy not to make fun of people."

I punched the Close Door button again, and the doors started to move together.

Stephanie jumped forward again and stopped the doors. "Come on, Diana. It's not that big a deal. We were just singing and having fun. Nobody thinks anything of it."

"Just leave me alone!" I said again.

As the doors closed a final time, she said, "What if I get her to apologize?"

I didn't answer. The elevator headed down to another floor, and then I realized I hadn't punched the deck number for our room yet. I punched in fourteen.

I stood in front of the doors, my stomach feeling queasy as the elevator dropped, and I realized I was shaking. I thought about what Dr. Shrink had told me. Take deep breaths. Moronic Mood-o-Meter at two.

The doors opened. I was on deck fourteen. I stepped out of the elevator but didn't know which way to go. I checked my jean pocket for my room card. I had it. But it didn't have the room number written on it. I wasn't sure I could remember the room number.

I looked at the map of the ship on the wall to try to figure out which hall to walk down and which way to go. I had gotten turned around and couldn't remember whether I had to go toward the back of the ship or the front.

I thought I chose the right direction and started heading down the narrow corridor. My heart was still beating wildly, and I could feel the flush on my cheeks. I wouldn't speak to Lauren for the rest of the trip, that was for sure. How could Stephanie ever have thought she was "awesome." She was so mean!

Pretty soon it seemed like the numbers on the doors weren't going in the right direction and so I turned around and went the other way down the corridor. I passed a few people, and they smiled and said hello.

Maybe Lauren was getting back at me for telling that they were making fun of the way Uncle Ted said "at the end of the day." I could tell she was mad about that. But so what. She and Stephanie had been making fun of him. It wasn't my job to keep their secret.

I looked at the numbers on the doors again. I'd gotten to another section of rooms. What was our room number? I had kind of forgotten.

I wondered where Mom was right now. She and Aunt Carol had stayed in the dining room when we left with Norm and Uncle Ted. Maybe all the grown-ups were still sitting there. I didn't want to see them really, but since I couldn't remember our room number, I probably needed to find them.

I wasn't going back to the teen club, that was for sure.

I stood in the hallway, undecided.

"Diana?"

I turned around and saw Grammy Verra walking down the hallway.

"Hi."

"Are you lost? This is my deck."

"Your deck?" I must have accidentally remembered Grammy's deck number instead of ours. "I can't remember my room number."

"We just finished talking and having coffee in the restaurant, and I was on my way back to my room," said Grammy. "I thought you girls were going to spend the evening in the teen club."

"Not me," I said. I couldn't keep the anger out of my voice.

"Oh," Grammy said, giving me a close look. "Come on, want to see my room? I have all the room numbers written down on a notepad. And you can go out on my balcony if you want to."

I hesitated. I didn't know Grammy Verra very well. But I didn't know where my room was, and I didn't know where Mom was. "Okay," I said.

I followed Grammy down the narrow corridor, then Grammy swiped her key card, and I followed her into her room. It was bigger than ours, with a king-size bed and a sliding-glass door that opened onto a balcony. A novel with a bookmark in it lay on the bedside table, and a pink satin robe lay across the bed.

"Check out my balcony. I'll find out your room number."

I pushed open the glass door and walked out onto the balcony, into the cool night air. The lights of the ship shone all around, and I could see people just below me, on a bigger balcony, sitting at a table drinking wine. Sounds of music from somewhere else on the ship wafted up. I could see the choppy waves down below in the cones of light cast from the ship. A rushing sound came from the movement of the ocean. Farther out to sea was blackness.

"Lovely, isn't it?" came Grammy Verra's voice.

"Yes."

"It would be nice to sit out here and talk," said Grammy. "We talk on the phone but I haven't really had a chance to get to know you so well in person, Diana." She sat in one of the two chairs arranged on the balcony and gestured for me to sit in the other one.

"There's not much to know about me."

"Oh, I bet that's not true," Grammy said. "Everyone has their own story."

I started to say, "I have to go," but for some reason I slid down into the other chair.

"Where did you grow up, Diana?"

"Mom and Dad and I used to live outside Washington, D.C." It made me feel sad to say it. "I lived there until I was in second grade, when they got divorced. Then Dad moved to Florida and Mom and I moved to Charlotte. And then, you know, Mom met Norm."

"And I'm so glad they did. Your mother has made my son very happy."

That was weird to think about. Norm was her son, like I was Mom's daughter.

"What do you think about living in the South?" she asked.

"I think people are too polite down here. They never say what they mean."

"That's an interesting observation. I like people to be direct too."

"And they move too slow."

Grammy Verra laughed. "Maybe you're right. The southern way of doing things. Maybe you'll just have to start taking your time more." She hesitated. "Do you have a close relationship with your grandparents?"

"On my dad's side, no. He doesn't get along with them. They live in Florida, but I've only seen them once or twice. It's always awkward."

"That's too bad."

"It doesn't matter."

"Sure it does. That's two people who could love you, and you could love them. What about your mom's side?"

"Neither of my grandparents are still alive."

"I'm sorry to hear that." Grammy hesitated. I could see her glasses glinting in the lights from the ship, but mostly her face was in darkness. "Well, three can be a crowd when it comes to girls. How are you and Lauren and Stephanie getting along?"

"We're not."

"What do you mean? Did something happen?"

I hesitated. I wasn't sure I trusted her. But the fact that I couldn't really see Grammy's face made it easier for me to talk. So I told Grammy Verra what had happened with Lauren.

"I never should have let them talk me into singing that stupid song," I finished.

"But you had fun singing the song, didn't you?"

"No."

"You didn't?"

"Not really." I knew I wasn't telling the truth, but I stubbornly stuck to my story. I had wanted to be part of what they were doing. And it had felt really good to be included.

But before that, they had talked about all of Uncle Ted's sayings, and I'd felt left out.

"Why did you tell at the dinner table about the girls making fun of Uncle Ted's sayings?"

"Well, they did it," I said.

"But you had to have known they didn't want Uncle Ted to know."

"Well, if they were doing it, he should know."

"How do you think they felt when you told?"

I shrugged. "I don't know. Embarrassed."

"And do you think that's what Lauren was doing—to get back at you and embarrass you?"

"I don't know. I don't want to talk about this anymore." She was saying that part of this was my own fault. It was starting to feel like one of my sessions with Dr. Shrink.

"Okay," said Grammy Verra. "I just wanted you to see that Lauren was doing the same thing you did. Not that either one of you was right. But when you lash out at another person, you might expect that some of the time that person will strike back and try to hurt you as much as you hurt them."

We sat in silence for a little while. My heart was beating hard. She was going to tell me to apologize, I knew it.

"As it turns out, Uncle Ted wasn't hurt, and he doesn't mind a little teasing. There's nothing wrong with a little light-spirited teasing."

"I'm not apologizing," I blurted out.

Grammy Verra was silent. "We have four more days together. It would be a shame if you girls keep on feuding and ruin your time on the cruise."

"I'll hang out with Luke," I said impulsively.

"I think he's met a couple of boys to play with."

The silence drew out between us. I could hear the movement of the water down below. I wondered what Grammy Verra thought of me. She probably thought I was a spoiled brat.

"I better get back to my room," I said. "Did you find the room numbers?"

"Yes." Grammy Verra got up and went back inside. I followed her into the room, where she gave me my room number and told me how to get there.

She stood in her doorway as I headed out. Even though she had been kind of hard on me, something made me want to hug her. But I held back and didn't.

6

STEPHANIE

Y ou embarrassed her, Lauren," I said, sliding into the chair next to her at the video-editing console. "Why can't you just apologize?"

Lauren was busy editing some of the footage she'd shot of Manuel when he had been folding towel animals in our room earlier. "She embarrassed *me*, talking about my dad's sayings right in front of him. She embarrassed you too, Steph!"

"Your dad didn't really seem to mind. He kind of

made a joke out of it." The chairs were swivel chairs, and I nervously turned myself around. "I just want everyone to get along."

"I know, Stephanie. You have always been Miss Fixit, always so worried about people being nice to each other." She stopped the shot at a still frame of Manuel and stared thoughtfully, then moved the image a few more frames forward.

"So? You make that sound like it's a bad thing."

"It's not bad. It's just, sometimes people don't agree."

"Well, why can't you apologize?" I said.

It had taken me awhile to talk to her about it. When Guy and I first walked back into the teen club after Diana left, karaoke was starting, and Lauren was already up on the stage picking a song.

"C'mon, let's you and me sing one!" Lauren had said, waving at me to come with her.

I hesitated. I was mad at her for what she'd done to Diana. I was mad at both of them.

"You do one, and I'll go next," I had said.

"C'mon, Steph, let's do one together," Lauren had insisted. I felt bad about staying at the teen club. When Diana left, I thought I should go after her. I felt like I was betraying her by staying with Lauren. But what Diana had done had embarrassed me too, and I didn't want to leave.

So I had gotten up and followed Lauren up on stage, watching the way she tossed back her long hair when she picked up the microphone.

We had looked at the list of songs, and Lauren and I had picked Taylor Swift's song "Sparks Fly." Guy and Evan watched us. When we sang the words "Kiss me on the sidewalk," we had started laughing and were kind of embarrassed. We ended up laughing the rest of the way through the song. It was a blast! I had left the stage feeling all flushed and excited.

"You guys have to do one too!" Lauren had said to the boys after we finished. They went up there, with Evan nervously straightening his collar (he wore his collar up, like a preppie) and Guy tossing his hair back several times. The two of them had decided on John Mayer's song "Half of My Heart."

The guys had messed up and forgotten the words even though they were printed right up on the screen, and we all started laughing.

We sat and watched a few other kids do karaoke. Then one girl started hogging the microphone, trying to do two songs in a row, and Josh had come up, taken the microphone, and turned off the speakers.

While that was happening, I had started thinking about the fact that I'd been so worried that Diana and Lauren would have a fight, and now they'd had one. It had happened. And now I needed to do something to help them make up. They couldn't be fighting for the rest of our trip! I couldn't imagine the painful silences in our tiny little room together.

So, anyway, now Lauren was sitting here editing some of the video she'd shot, and I was trying to convince her to apologize to Diana.

"I'm not going to apologize," she said. "Not unless Diana apologizes first."

"Why are you being so stubborn?"

Lauren shrugged. "I guess because I don't think I was wrong."

"You embarrassed her!"

"If I'd showed video of you singing 'Aweemaway,' would you have gotten mad?"

I twirled around in my chair again, thinking. "I would have been mortified but would have laughed it off."

"See?"

"But Diana's different."

Lauren looked at me levelly. "Why do you care so much about her anyway?"

"I care the same about you. I'm going to try to get her to apologize to you too."

"Like I said, if she apologizes first, I'll apologize," Lauren said.

The boys, who had been playing video games, came over and interrupted us. "Hey," said Evan, "do y'all want to go to the 'Movie Under the Stars' that's showing in a couple of nights? It's *Pirates of the Caribbean*."

"Sure," I said.

Lauren picked up her camera. "Hey, I have an idea. Let's wander around the ship and find interesting things to videotape. What if we found someone stowing away or something like that?"

"It would be easy to stow away on one of these ships," said Evan. "You could go through the buffet line ten times a day, and no one would know. They don't check your ID or anything."

"Where would you sleep?" I asked.

"You could sleep out by the pool, on a lounge chair. Or maybe on one of the sofas you see sitting around," said Evan.

"Where would you shower?" I said.

"Just go swimming every day," said Guy.

"How would you get on board in the first place? They check your passport and everything," Lauren pointed out.

"If you had a passport, I bet you could get on," said Evan.

"I bet a lot of people try it," said Guy. "Want to go searching for stowaways?"

"Now?" I hesitated. My heart started beating hard. The teen club would close in an hour. I was pretty sure Daddy and Uncle Ted were expecting us to stay in the club rather than wander around the ship.

"Yeah!" said Lauren. "I've been dying to try to find my way around."

"I want to check out the rock-climbing wall," said Evan. "What about you guys?"

I didn't want to sound like a baby or a goody-goody and be the only one who didn't want to leave the teen club. So when they got their stuff and got ready to leave, I did too.

As we were leaving, Josh came up to us. "You guys heading out? Were your parents going to come back for you or what?"

"No, they just said to come back to the room when we were ready," Lauren said.

"Okay, cool. Take it easy; maybe I'll see you tomorrow," he said.

"Let's walk on the upper deck," said Evan. We went up two flights of stairs and came out on the upper deck. As we stepped out into the open, the breeze blew our hair and plastered our shirts against our skin.

"Wow, look at the stars!" I said. They were brilliant, spread across the sky like bright diamonds. The movement of the water all around us created a constant wall of sound.

Evan was walking along with Lauren, and I was walking along with Guy.

I started asking Guy about what it was like to be diabetic.

"It's a definite challenge," he said. "I found out I had diabetes when I was seven. I had to start testing my blood sugar then. When you're diabetic, your body doesn't make its own insulin, so you have to give it to yourself."

"Do you have to stick yourself?"

"Yes, but the needles are so tiny, you can barely feel it. It doesn't hurt. You have to learn about blood sugar and what kinds of foods cause it to go up or down, and you have to test your blood sugar about five or six times a day."

"What kinds of foods cause your blood sugar to go up?"

"Sweets and carbohydrates. Carbohydrates get metabolized into sugar, so you have to watch the carbohydrates you eat … like pizza or chips. Eating a lot of snack food isn't good. One thing that's really good for you if you're diabetic is exercise. It burns up the glucose. But at the same time, you have to be careful not to let your blood sugar get too low."

"Wow." I hadn't ever thought about having to watch so closely everything I ate and did. I thought about the times we had cheerleading practice and did back tucks until we were about to throw up. None of us worried about our blood sugar. It was a different way of living.

Guy shrugged. "When I was first diagnosed, I felt really sorry for myself. I thought, *why did this have to happen to me?* But you get used to it. If my blood sugar is high, I need to give myself more insulin. If my blood sugar is low, like after exercising, I need to eat or drink something with sugar in it. Like, I just sip Gatorade during soccer practice to keep my blood sugar from falling. I'm not going to let it keep me from doing stuff. I want to play Division I soccer in college, and I'm not going to give that up. I'm not going to let it beat me."

"That's great," I said. I really admired him for that.

"And it's kind of changed the way I think about the whole world. If I wanted to rebel and not test myself, the only person I'd be hurting would be me. It made me grow up and take responsibility for myself faster. And I've noticed that sometimes I feel more protective of kids that are younger than me."

I sneaked a look at him when he said that. I hadn't met many boys who talked about responsibility. He had a softness and wistfulness to his face that I liked.

We walked around the ship and talked for an hour. The adults had gone to a show, and when the show let out, we saw some of the performers in their dance costumes. They were friendly and spoke with all sorts of different accents. By then it was close to our eleven-o'clock curfew, and so we had to say good-bye to the boys. Evan gave us a salute and said maybe they'd see us tomorrow at the teen club or around the boat. Guy said good-bye and then lightly touched my arm. I felt a little tingle when he did that.

When Lauren and I got back to the room, Diana was already curled up on her bunk, asleep. I tried to talk quietly so I wouldn't wake her. We were kind of gig-gling about the boys, because Evan was such a mama's boy. We had been kidding him and asking if his mom ironed his underwear.

What an amazing first day on the cruise! Except for Lauren and Diana's fight, of course.

The next morning when I woke up, Lauren was still asleep and Diana was gone. I wondered if she'd gone to the buffet for breakfast, and I wanted to try and talk to her. So I got up quietly, got dressed, and tiptoed out.

When I got to the buffet, I looked around at the tables, and what did I see but Diana eating breakfast with Grammy Verra! I suddenly felt jealous. I realized they were both allowed to do whatever they wanted, but I felt a little strange. Diana wasn't even Grammy Verra's real granddaughter—but they were sitting together talking like they were best friends. I had always thought I was Grammy Verra's favorite!

The buffet was overwhelming. There was every kind of breakfast cereal, bagel and muffin, and fruits of all kinds, just rows of them in all colors like rainbows. There was sausage and an omelette bar. There were pancakes and waffles. There were blintzes, and I didn't even know what those were! Finally I got a plain omelette with cheese and joined Diana and Grammy Verra. I should have guessed what they'd be talking about: animals. Grammy Verra was telling Diana about her little dog, Botticelli, or Jelly for short.

"So, anyway, when Jelly wants a treat, he'll stand up on his hind legs and move his short little front legs up and down like he's begging," Grammy was saying. "His eyes are big and brown, and they just implore you. It's so adorable, how can I deny him anything?"

"Grammy's dog is the most spoiled dog in the world," I said as I put my tray down on the table. "She gives him everything he wants."

"Well, and he's very smart too. He knows at least twenty words," Grammy said.

"He knows his name, as well as *toy, walk, treat, out, down, sit, stay,* ..."

"Grammy, he never sits or stays," I said. "He never does anything you tell him to do."

"That's just because he's so smart. He's too smart to be bossed around."

"Too spoiled, you mean," I said, laughing.

"He's not going to like knowing that you talked about him like that, Stephanie!" Grammy teased. "You better be careful. He is my precious little boy, is what he is. I wish I could have brought him on the cruise. He keeps me company."

"I know, Grammy. I'm just giving you a hard time about him."

"Diana and I have been having some nice talks, haven't we, Diana?" Grammy said. "I'm enjoying getting to know her better."

"That's great," I said, feeling jealous again but smiling at Diana. She gave a small smile. I didn't know whether it was sarcastic or not.

"She's been telling me about her horse, Commanche," Grammy went on.

"Well, he's not my horse. He's the horse I ride when I go to the barn," Diana explained to Grammy. "I told her that Commanche sticks his head out when I come into the barn. He knows my walk," said Diana.

"Isn't that great when an animal knows us? It makes us feel good, doesn't it?" Grammy said.

"Yeah!" Diana said.

She and Grammy both nodded and laughed. I told

myself that Grammy was just trying to get to know Diana. And I knew Diana wasn't close to her real grandparents. After that, Daddy and Lynn came and joined us, and then Aunt Carol and Uncle Ted and Luke, so we were all scooting over and making room for people to put their trays on the table, and the conversation was like a three-ring circus. Lauren was the only one who wasn't there. I figured she was still sleeping. I was worried about what would happen when she and Diana saw each other.

"You girls better go claim spots by the pool before it gets too late," Daddy said.

I stood up. "Okay, I'm going. Diana, want to come find a spot out by the pool?"

Diana shrugged. "I guess so."

"We're going to go to the quiet adult pool," said Lynn. "You girls are welcome to sit with us or go to the young people's pool and play games."

"Young people's pool!" I said excitedly.

When we got back to the room, Lauren lay with her face turned toward the wall while Diana and I put on our swimsuits.

"Want me to try to save a chair for you, Lauren?" I asked.

"Okay," she mumbled.

Diana didn't say anything.

It was a beautiful day, with blue skies above dotted with scattered clouds and the deep-green water surrounding us as far as we could see in every direction. When we looked over the edge of the deck, we could see the lacy, white foam spreading out behind the ship from the engines.

Diana and I claimed lounge chairs far enough away from the pool that we wouldn't get splashed. I put a towel on the lounge chair on the other side of me for Lauren. I was nervous but also still mad that they weren't speaking to each other.

I lay on my lounge chair and put on my suntan lotion. Mama let me get a new bikini that's a hot-pink-and-yellow print, and I loved it. Diana was still wearing a faded navy-blue Speedo that she had worn for swim team last year. Lynn had offered to take her shopping for a new bathing suit, and Diana said she'd rather go to the barn. I wished I understood her!

"Good morning, this is your captain speaking" came a deep accented voice over the loudspeaker system. "Today we're at sea, and we will be sailing at a speed of fourteen knots per hour. We should arrive at port in Grand Cayman by early tomorrow morning. It's seventy-eight degrees on board today. In New York it's thirty degrees. Enjoy your day at sea!"

"It's hard to believe it's so cold at home," I said to

Diana. "If it's thirty degrees in New York, it's probably somewhere in the forties in North Carolina."

"The horses are probably wearing blankets in their stalls," she said.

Now was my chance to talk to Diana about apologizing. I hesitated, then plunged ahead on. "Hey, Lauren said she'd apologize for showing the video of you last night if you apologize for telling about our conversation about Uncle Ted's sayings."

Diana shot me an angry look. "But you guys are the ones that talked about it."

"I know, but we really didn't want Uncle Ted to know. It was embarrassing when you did that."

"He didn't get mad."

"He could've. And you don't know if his feelings were hurt or not."

Diana played with the fringe on her beach bag. "Lauren *really* embarrassed me. And she did it on purpose."

"I think she did it because you hurt her feelings first," I said. "If both of you just say you're sorry, we can get on with our fabulous trip."

Diana looked out into the distance for what seemed like a long time. "It just really hurt my feelings."

"So now you know how it feels," I said.

Diana drew a deep breath. "Okay. I'll apologize if she apologizes."

"Whew!" I drew my hand across my brow to show I'd been sweating it out. "That's great. It's the right thing to do. So you'll apologize when she comes out?"

"Yes."

Evan and Guy came out then, and so we hung around with them. Diana was usually shy with boys, and today was no different. Guy and Evan were both kind of talking to me. I tried a couple of times to pull her into the conversation.

"So, Diana is the number-one girl on our cross-country team," I told Guy. "She leaves the other girls in her dust."

"No kidding; that's cool," Guy said.

Diana smiled nervously. "I like running."

"I ran cross-country last year, but this year I played soccer. Still a boatload of running," Evan said.

"Wait, Evan, we were talking about Diana," Guy said. "So, tell us more about being on cross-country, Diana."

I was so impressed. I had never seen a boy do that— shift attention to another person that way. I watched the way Guy sat forward and focused on Diana, and I thought, *Wow, he's a nice guy.*

"Oh, I didn't even want to do it at first," Diana said. "My stepfather made me."

"Your stepfather?" Guy asked. "That's kind of cool."

"Yeah. Then I started liking it." Diana shrugged.

I was happy that Diana had said something good about Daddy. There was a time when I thought she never would.

A waiter came around with sodas and snacks.

"Did you see that guy over there?" Guy said to me. "He was at the teen club last night. He just tried to order a beer."

We all watched as the waiter asked for the guy's ID and then refused him service.

When Lauren finally came out, Diana glanced at her and then looked away, and Lauren at first talked only to me and the guys. Lauren was wearing a brand-new red-and-white bikini, and I could see Evan and Guy paying attention when she took off her cover-up.

Waiting for Diana to apologize, I held my breath. I was afraid she wouldn't do it in front of Evan and Guy. I could see her nervously playing with the fringe on her beach bag again. The air between the three of us hung thick and heavy.

Diana cleared her throat. "Hey, Lauren."

"Yeah?"

"I'm sorry about telling about Uncle Ted's sayings last night. I see now that it embarrassed you guys."

"It did. I couldn't believe you told on us on purpose."

I held my breath. Lauren was supposed to apologize now, not give Diana a hard time.

"I didn't mean to embarrass you," Diana said again. Her face was turning red. "Like I said, I'm sorry."

"Okay … thanks," Lauren said.

I held my breath. Lauren had to apologize now!

She sighed like she was annoyed. "I'm sorry I showed the video of you singing and skipping at the teen club last night."

"I was so embarrassed," Diana said. "It really hurt my feelings."

"Well, in my opinion, if you can't take a little joke—"

"Lauren!" I said. "You said you'd apologize. Don't argue about it anymore."

Lauren looked down and examined her nail polish. "Okay. I'm sorry. I shouldn't have done that."

"Okay … thanks," Diana said.

I stood up. "Okay! Apologies are done! Now we can go back to having fun. And you girls, please don't make me have to do that again. We need to get along! Who wants to go swimming?"

I made both of them get in the water with me, and in a few minutes, it seemed to me that everyone was getting along all right.

I was happy they had apologized. But I knew how stubborn they both were. Had it seemed too easy?

7

DIANA

I hadn't apologized very many times in my life for things I'd done, and I felt kind of awkward, so after an hour or so sitting out by the pool, I decided to go up to the track at the back of the ship for a run. Lauren kept videotaping everyone, and she and Stephanie wanted to keep flirting with the boys, so I decided I should just leave.

Mom and Norm told me it was fine to go to the track by myself, so I headed back to our room to get my running shoes. But while I was in the hall outside the room, I overheard our cabin steward, Manuel, in the room across the hall with the cleaning supplies, talking to someone else in a hissed whisper.

"I am just not sure I want to do it!" Manuel said. "What if we get caught?"

"You can't change your mind now!" said the other voice with an American accent. I couldn't see what the man looked like. "I'm counting on you. You said you were desperate for the money."

I stood very still, holding my key card, waiting for them to talk more.

"I am. For my little boy."

"Then you'll do it."

There was silence after that. Someone left the supply room, and I didn't turn around to see what he looked like. I went into my room and put on my running shorts and shoes, wondering what Manuel and the other guy were talking about doing.

When I came back out of the room, I peeked into the cleaning-supply room, but Manuel was gone. I stood around for a little bit, waiting to see if he'd come back, but he didn't. I had figured out how to get to the track, by going toward the back of the ship, so I headed back that way and took the elevator to the top floor. When I stepped out of the elevator, I was outside on the top deck, and a stiff, warm breeze blew my hair around. I started out running, wondering again what that argument I'd overheard had been all about. Something they didn't want to get caught doing, so it must be illegal. Strange. I wondered if I should tell Stephanie about it.

I loved running. Finding out that I was the fastest girl on the cross-country team had done things for me. It became like an identity for me. I had more confidence about other things because I was good at running. And people were nicer to me. I felt cynical about that, because shouldn't people be nice no matter what, whether you can win a race or not? Sometimes I wanted to say to people, "Hey, how come you weren't nice to me last year before I was on the cross-country team? What's really changed about who I am?" But at the same time, it felt good to be treated better. To feel more like I belonged.

Some kids still called me "annn-i-mal." But having the respect of the cross-country team gave me more courage and strength to ignore what those other people said.

While I was running, I could let my mind wander. Things that had been bothering me before I ran somehow worked themselves out while I was running. I could solve problems. I could work out anger. I had found out that when my Moronic Mood-o-Meter was at a seven or above, I could go for a run and come back out of breath but feeling calm and relaxed. Running seemed to help my brain waves.

So while I was running on that little track, looking out at the water all around, I thought through my fight with Lauren and our awkward apologies. There really hadn't been a reason for me to tell on Stephanie and Lauren. I had just done it to be spiteful, I admitted it. And once Lauren tried to get back at me, I realized how hard the whole situation was for Stephanie, trying to mediate between us. And I decided I would try harder to get along with Lauren. After all, this was a fantastic trip, and we were lucky to be here. It would be stupid to ruin it with bickering.

After my run I walked around the track a few times, cooling off, just thinking about how amazing it was to be out in the middle of all this water. My shirt and hair were damp, but in the sea breeze, the sweat dried. The sun reflected off the shifting surfaces of the waves, and the moving water had an amazing aura—a deep rushing background sound that was soothing.

On my way back, I stopped by the adult pool. It was so boring and different from our pool! The grown-ups lay around quietly reading or sleeping in the sun. A lot of the grown-ups were drinking tall drinks with umbrellas in them. No one was even in the pool, and its surface was almost still. Mom and Norm were sitting with Uncle Ted, Aunt Carol, and Grammy Verra, talking about what would happen tomorrow when we docked at Grand Cayman.

I sat on the edge of Mom's lounge chair, thinking again about what I'd overheard Manuel saying. I decided I'd tell Stephanie, but not the grown-ups.

"Grand Cayman is supposed to have some of the best snorkeling in the world, because there are so few ocean currents. The water is supposed to be amazingly clear. You can snorkel right off the public beach," said Norm. He had a guidebook open. "The kids will get a kick out of seeing all the fish around the coral reef. And there's this place called Stingray City where there are dozens of tame stingrays in about three feet of water, and you can feed them. Should we go there?"

"Yes!" I said. Feeding stingrays sounded amazing. "Are you going, Grammy Verra?"

"No, I think I'll stay on the boat and get a spa treatment or something," she said. "Too much hullabaloo getting on and off the boat for me."

I went back to the young people's pool determined to get along better with everyone. When I got there, Luke, Evan, and Guy, and several other boys were playing basketball in the pool, and the splashing was so bad that Lauren and Stephanie had moved their stuff farther away from the pool. But they hadn't saved a chair for me this time.

"That's okay," Stephanie said. "Sit on the edge of my chair, Diana."

At that minute I felt like leaving. It was amazing how I had been thinking so hard about getting along, and then one little thing happened, and I felt like giving up on everything and going back to the room.

"Or ... wait a minute," Lauren said, standing up. And she went over to the other side of the pool and asked someone if she could have one of the lounges next to them. She grabbed the chair and dragged it all the way back. "Here," she said.

"Wow, that was nice, Lauren," said Stephanie.

"Yeah, thanks," I said. It was cool that Lauren was trying to be nice to me. I sat on the chair in my running stuff. "Hey, guess what," I said.

"What?"

"I overheard our cabin steward having the weirdest conversation," I said. And then I told them what I had overheard.

"That is scary," Stephanie agreed. "They're going to do something illegal to make money."

"That's what it sounds like," Lauren said. "Hey, I have an idea. I'll ask Manuel if I can interview him on video-tape, and then maybe we'll find out what's going on."

"That's a good idea," Stephanie said. "But you'll have to be careful not to act suspicious about anything."

"I've got a great poker face," Lauren assured us.

She got excited about doing the interview, and so after lunch at the buffet, we went in search of Manuel. We found him in the hallway a few doors down from our room with a cart full of clean towels.

"Hello, girls," he said with a ready smile. His uniform was perfectly clean and ironed. "How is your cruise going so far?"

"Just great," Lauren said, cradling her camera. "We were wondering, could we interview you? I have to do a project for school since I'm missing a few days to come on this trip."

Manuel's broad face clouded with doubt for a moment, but then his smile returned. "Sure," he said. "That would be fine. How long will it take?"

"Maybe fifteen minutes," Lauren said.

A few minutes later, he was sitting in the desk chair in our stateroom, and Lauren sat on the bed with the camera aimed at him.

"How long have you been working for the cruise line?"

"For five years."

"How do you like it?"

He smiled broadly. "I love working for the cruise line. It is hard work but a good job."

"What is your job like?"

"I am a cabin steward, and twice a day I clean and straighten the cabins of my customers. I assist with luggage and try to give my customers good service. I try in every way I can to make their trip pleasant. I do not have many days off. I know how to fold towel animals!"

"What is your favorite part of the job?"

"I enjoy meeting all the people. I get to meet people from all over the world. It helps you to understand that there is more to life than the place where you are from. I love learning about new places."

"Do you have a roommate here on the ship?"

"Yes, I share a room with Ryan, another steward. He is an American from California."

"Is your cabin like this room?"

Manuel shook his head. "Much smaller. But we are working all the time, and we do not spend very much time in our rooms."

"We don't spend much time in here either," Stephanie said, agreeing.

"Have there been any crimes committed on any of your trips?" Lauren asked this question casually. I couldn't believe she dared to ask it!

Manuel hesitated. "What do you mean?" he asked.

Did he seem guilty? I couldn't look at him.

"I don't know," Lauren said. "Like stowaways or people being arrested or anything like that."

"Yes, we did have a stowaway once. It was a woman. They caught her when she was disembarking at the end of the cruise."

"How did she get away with it?"

"She acted like a passenger, I was told." Manuel crossed his arms over his chest. "And then there have been passengers arrested for smuggling drugs and things like that."

"Really?" Lauren stared at Manuel and waited for him to say more. My heart was pounding so hard, I was sure that someone must be able to hear it.

"Yes," Manuel said. "It was good that they were caught."

We all nodded and agreed. I still couldn't look at him. I could hardly breathe.

"I will tell you about the most exciting trip I have made," Manuel said suddenly. "Once we were sailing through rough weather, and the ship was rocking and tables and chairs went sliding across the room, and dishes slid off of tables and broke everywhere. It was pretty scary. I was happy to get into safer waters! I called my wife that night in great relief, and it was so good to hear my children's voices." Manuel's face broke wide in a smile of relief as he remembered.

"Where does your family live?"

"My family lives in Manila, Philippines."

"How often do you see your family?"

"I am on the ship for ten months, and then I have two months off to spend with my family."

"Is that hard?"

Manuel nodded. "Yes, it can be hard. I have four children, and I was not able to be there for the birth of two of them."

"Oh no!" Stephanie said.

Now Manuel hesitated and looked at his hands. He reached into his pocket and pulled out the key chain with the photographs on it that we had seen before. He held it up for the camera. "This is my family ... my wife, Paloma, and Francisco is five, Sandra is four, Raul is three, and Carlo is two. And recently we found out that Carlo, my youngest son, is deaf. Because of my job, I was not there to talk to the doctors."

"He's deaf?"

"Yes, he was sick with a high fever, and as a result he lost most of his hearing. Now he needs hearing aids. You cannot imagine what it is like to tell your son you love him, and he does not understand." Manuel quickly looked away from Lauren and put his hand over his mouth.

"When will he get the hearing aids?"

"When we are able to save the money, we will be able to get the aids. I am saving as much as I can now. They are very expensive. But as a parent you will do anything for your child. And it is hard not being there. My wife is heroic." Then he shrugged and smiled. "It is a challenge, but I am lucky to have this job. And I keep up with the kids on Skype. Last night my daughter Sandra sang 'Itsy Bitsy Spider' to me over Skype." He demonstrated the finger motions for "Itsy Bitsy Spider." "And I will be home again in just a few weeks. I must have faith that we will be able to get the money for Carlo."

The moment stretched out as Manuel smiled into the camera. He had a look of trust and hope on his face. After a beat, Lauren asked him some more questions about traveling, and then he demonstrated how to fold several towels into monkey shapes.

"Well, thanks for letting us interview you!" Stephanie said.

"You are welcome. Thank you for taking the time to talk with me. And I will hope to see you around the boat." After Manuel left, the three of us sat on our beds in silence, staring at each other.

"He's so nice. I can't believe he's doing something illegal," Stephanie said.

"Could you have imagined what you heard? Or

maybe you thought it was him and it was someone else?" Lauren asked.

I immediately felt a flush of anger. "No, Lauren, I didn't imagine it! And yes, I'm sure it was him!"

"I'm sorry, I'm sorry," Lauren quickly said. "I just can't imagine him doing anything wrong."

"Me, either," I said. Now that Lauren had apologized, I carefully reviewed the scene I had heard in my head, wondering if I might have heard it wrong.

"But we did find out that he needs money," Lauren said. "For the hearing aids."

"Well, there's one more thing," I said. "Manuel said he has an American roommate, and the other guy I heard talking has an American accent."

"There are a lot of people on this ship with American accents," Lauren said.

"Well, there's nothing else we can do," Stephanie said. "Except just watch and listen whenever he's around and see if we can find out anything else."

Had I imagined it? Had it been another steward? Had I just thought it was Manuel? I lay on my bunk, beginning to doubt everything I thought I'd heard.

8

STEPHANIE

"Group seven, please come to the boarding area. Group seven, to the boarding area."

Everyone in our family, except Grammy, sat in the auditorium at the front of the ship in our bathing suits with our beach bags. Over a loudspeaker, the cruise director called groups one at a time to come forward. Our ship was now docked in the Grand Cayman harbor, and we were waiting to board the tender to go onto the island. The harbor wasn't deep enough for our cruise ship, so we had to dock out by the mouth of a bay, and small groups of us would ride small passenger boats called tenders to the dock.

"I am so excited!" Lauren said, poking my knee with hers. "Aren't you?"

"Yeah!" I couldn't wait to see the island. Lynn had told us that Grand Cayman was a British territory, and so the people spoke with an accent similar to the British accent, and they drove on the left. When the Cayman Islands were first discovered by Christopher Columbus, they were called Las Tortugas because of the many sea turtles that were seen there. On the island was a sea turtle farm owned by the government, called Boatswain's Beach, where captive green sea turtles were bred. In October every year was a special event where hundreds of turtles were released into the wild. Lynn had said that now some of the mature green sea turtles were coming back to lay their eggs on the beach near the turtle farm. The Grand Cayman flag as well as several of the Grand Cayman coins featured the sea turtle.

I was a little scared to go snorkeling. What if I saw a big fish? What if I saw a shark? I hadn't mentioned being scared to anyone, and no one else acted like it was bothering them. I knew what Daddy would say. He was always pooh-poohing my fears. I had taken off all my jewelry because I had heard that bright, sparkly things can attract fish like barracuda.

I sat between Diana and Lauren on one of the auditorium seats. That was the way we seemed to go everywhere, with me in the middle, like I was the only connection between them. Both of them talked to me but not much to each other. Yet both of them had been careful not to do or say anything mean to each other ever since they apologized. I had been praying for help keeping the peace. Of course, we still had three days to go!

I had looked for Evan and Guy and their families but didn't see them. They had told us that they were going scuba diving. Probably their group had left earlier than this.

The whole situation with Manuel was strange. I didn't want to doubt what Diana had said, but could she have made a mistake? Was she just trying to get attention? He seemed like such a nice person. And he sounded like he was such a caring father to all of those little children. I had just about decided that what we ought to do was forget about what she thought she'd overheard.

"Group nine; please come to the boarding area. Group nine, to the boarding area."

"That's us!" Daddy said. He put his arm around

Lynn and waved us toward the exit to the tender. We filed off the ship and into the bright sunshine, and then climbed onto the small passenger boat bobbing beside the ship. The boat had rows of benches, and we filled it up. Then the boat's motor started up. As we puttered across the bay, the wind blew in our hair and the waves lapped against the sides of the boat. The sun bore down on us, and the water beneath us was so clear we could see the white sand on the bottom below.

"A short walk to George Town and shopping, and that way is Seven Mile Beach," said the tender captain as we tied up at a dock.

We headed for the beach and saw a long, beautiful stretch of white sand lined with small, colorful hotels and buildings, lounge chairs in lines, and palm and coconut trees swaying in the breeze. Hibiscus plants, adorned with big red-and-yellow blossoms, dotted the landscape. Grouped on the sand were sailboats, kayaks, Jet Skis, and other aquatic equipment.

"Wow!" Lauren said. "It's beautiful here!"

"And see out there," said Uncle Ted, pointing toward the water at dark shadows beneath the surface a few dozen yards from the beach. "That's a coral reef where you can snorkel and see all kinds of fish. I used to own a saltwater tank when I was young, and I used to have all these beautiful brightly colored fish."

"I didn't know that," said Aunt Carol. "When did you have that?"

"Before I knew you, my dear," said Uncle Ted. "When I had my swinging bachelor pad."

Aunt Carol and Lynn laughed at that. "Oh, I can just imagine," said Aunt Carol.

"I had a trigger fish and a queen angel, a royal gramma fish, a yellow tang, and a blue tang. And a tomato clown fish like Nemo. I loved that tank," said Uncle Ted. "I named all my fish."

"Aha!" said Aunt Carol, laughing. "So instead of inviting women over to see your etchings, you invited them over to see Nemo and his friends."

"Yes, all the myriad of women I dated," said Uncle Ted, chuckling.

We walked down the beach toward the area where Daddy had read the snorkeling would be good.

"I can't wait to snorkel!" said Luke. "I wish we could scuba."

"I wish I had an underwater camera," said Lauren.

"I don't have to snorkel," I said.

"Oh, honey, of course you do," Daddy said, putting his arm around me. "You don't want to miss out on an adventure like that. Imagine coming to Grand Cayman and not going snorkeling!"

I knew he'd be that way. I decided not to say anything

else. Part of me did want to try it. Later, when I talked to Guy about our day on Grand Cayman, I wanted to be able to tell him that I'd snorkeled. Another part of me was scared, but I had told myself that I wasn't going to let my fears get the best of me on this trip. I wanted to be brave like Diana!

It was easy to find a place that rented snorkel equipment. A young man from Grand Cayman who worked there pointed out the sizes of the flippers and masks.

"For small feet or small faces, you should choose these over here," he said, with a slight British accent, as he held up smaller flippers and masks. Trying on the various flipper sizes was so funny; Lauren, Luke, and I walked around taking big awkward steps, like ducks. Diana even laughed. All of us finally found a good fit.

"I'll stay with the stuff while the rest of you snorkel," said Aunt Carol. And so she set the beach bags on lounge chairs while the rest of us carried our snorkel equipment down to the water.

"Everybody make sure they have a snorkeling buddy," Daddy said.

Diana and Lauren both wanted to be buddies with me, but I wanted to make sure I was snorkeling near Daddy and Lynn. I put on the flippers and followed Daddy and Lynn through the gentle breakers out into the water about waist deep. The water was refreshing but not too cold—just perfect—and the clear waves rolling into the beach were small. The sun was so bright, sparkling off the surface of the water. It was almost like a dream.

"See how calm the water is," Daddy said. "Great visibility underwater."

"Girls, you're supposed to spit in your mask and rub the spit around the inside surface in order to keep your mask from fogging up," Lynn said.

"Eww!" Lauren said.

"I know, it's kind of gross, but it's what you're supposed to do."

"And then tighten the mask strap after you put it on so that it doesn't leak." She showed us how to do that.

Finally I got the mask on, then pushed off, kicking with my flippers and looking at the sandy ocean floor below me. I kicked into deeper water and headed toward the darkness of the coral reef ahead. I could hear my own loud breathing through the snorkel. The deeper water felt colder, and I had a little chill, but I could see Daddy and Lynn out of the corner of my eye, and I could hear the bubbles coming from their snorkels, so I kept kicking.

Soon I was floating on top of the water with the green edge of the coral reef below me. I watched the fronds of the water plants sway in the waves, and gradually I could see dozens of small, colorful fish darting in and out of the coral. They were such bright colors! One of them was like a big yellow coin, round and flat, with a tail fin. Another was pinkish with gigantic eyes. One was shaped like a pen, and it was half purple and half yellow—amazing! Another looked like Nemo from *Finding Nemo* — orange with round flippers and white stripes across its eyes. I floated on top of the water, listening to myself breathe and watching Daddy and Lynn as they dove down and pointed out the fish. The underwater sounds were so cool.

Just then I saw a long silver fish swimming along the top not too far from me. Was that a barracuda? My heart started pounding, and I heard the bubbles racing out of my snorkel. I struggled to straighten up in the water, surfacing and grabbing for Daddy's arm.

"What, Steph?" Daddy surfaced, pulling his mask from his face, out of breath. "What's the matter?"

I pointed at the long thin fish.

"That's not a barracuda," he said. "Just a needlefish. It's okay. Keep snorkeling."

I took a deep breath. It sure looked like a barracuda. But I put my mask back on and looked down at the coral. I took another breath, trying to calm myself. Schools of white fish with black-and-yellow stripes wove and darted through the small crevices of the coral. A majestic blue fish with some yellow markings, shaped like a dinner plate, floated from behind a plant whose branches looked like long dark fingers. A delicately patterned sea fan moved ever so slightly in the current.

Diana swam over to me waving and pointing down. I looked down on the sandy bottom and saw a big reddish starfish. I held my thumbs up to show her I'd seen it.

It was truly a whole different world. I kept getting little chills down my spine.

Eventually Lauren, Diana, and I swam back to shore, then ran, dripping and out of breath, to rest on the lounge chairs where Aunt Carol and Lynn were sitting.

"That was so cool," Diana said. "You know what I wish I could do? I wish I could ride on the beach here."

"I think they do have a stable somewhere on the island," Lynn said. "But we only have one day here, so we don't have time to ride on this trip." She adjusted her sunglasses and turned a page in the guidebook. "The Cayman Islands are home to several endangered species of animals," she said.

"Like what?" said Diana eagerly.

"There are the green sea turtles. Do you girls want to go to the turtle farm?" Lynn asked, turning the pages. "It says here that over thirty thousand turtles from the farm have been released into the wild. But it says that sixty percent of the turtles on the farm are for consumption."

"Consumption?" said Diana with a gasp. "Do you mean to *eat?*"

"Yes, I think that's what it means," Lynn said. "The other forty percent of the turtles are chosen for breeding and release. There's a big day in October—they must have just had it a few weeks ago—when they have a big release party and release hundreds of turtles into the wild each year."

"I can't believe it! That the turtle farm raises the turtles to be eaten. That's horrible. I don't want to go there!"

I wondered how the turtle-farm operators chose which turtles were to be bred and which were to be eaten. I agreed with Diana, it did sound horrible.

"I think they had turtle soup on one of the menus in George Town," said Aunt Carol.

"Oh no! That's horrendous!" Diana said. "I'm going to boycott that restaurant. How can they do that? In fact, I want to become a vegetarian."

"Being a vegetarian isn't easy," said Aunt Carol. "You have to learn a lot about nutrition. And it may not be a good idea to become one before you're an adult, while you still have growing to do."

I supposed Aunt Carol was right. It made me think of Guy and how careful he had to be with what he ate as a diabetic.

"The guidebook says that keeping turtles on ships was one way historically that sailors were able to have fresh meat when they were at sea for a long time," Lynn said. "And it also says that the people of the Cayman Islands have been eating turtles for five hundred years, and it's often hard to change the way people think about cultural customs like that."

"What other animals are endangered?" Diana asked.

"Let's see," said Lynn. "There is a certain kind of parrot called a Cayman Brac parrot that's endangered. Cayman Brac is the only place in the world it's found. There were about five hundred of them in the world before the last hurricane hit the Caymans, and now the numbers are at about three hundred, the book says."

"What does it look like?"

"It's got a green body and brilliant blue wing feathers. It has red cheeks and black ears, apparently. There is a parrot preserve on Cayman Brac. And there is a type of iguana called a blue iguana, and the Cayman Islands are the only place where it's found. It says it's one of the rarest breed of iguanas in the world. The blue iguana can grow to over five feet long. This guidebook calls them magnificent creatures. There is a research and breeding facility for the blue iguana here on Grand Cayman. They saved it from extinction. I remember feeding an iguana once when I was on Saint Thomas many years ago," Lynn said.

"What did it eat?"

"Hibiscus flowers. It seemed to love them. And it chewed very slowly. The flower would very gradually get pulled into its mouth. They seem like very gentle lizards. I came to think of this one that liked to sit on a rock beside our hotel patio as a pet. I would always look for it when we went outside."

"Wow," said Diana. "Were you with Dad then?"

"Yes," Lynn said quickly. "It was before you were born." I had noticed that Lynn didn't really like to talk about the time she was married to Diana's dad.

"Isn't it amazing there are so many animals that are only found here on the Cayman Islands?" said Aunt Carol.

"I think there is a geographical reason for islands to have endangered species, when you think about it," said Lynn.

Finally Daddy and Uncle Ted and Luke came out of the water.

"Wow! That was just gorgeous snorkeling," said Daddy, dropping his mask and fins on the sand, then straightening the towel on his lounge chair. "I don't know when I've seen water so clear."

"So, what'd you think, Luke?" Aunt Carol asked.

"The needlefish are cool," he said. "They look like barracudas."

"I know!" I said. "I thought that's what they were!"

After getting dried off, we took the boat to Stingray City. Stingray City was a place where the stingrays were tame, and we were able to swim among them. We stood in the chest-deep water, and the stingrays swam around us, flapping their fins to propel themselves through the water like Batman. The stingrays were big, as big as a round plastic sled. Diana reached out and touched one and said that on top the skin felt rough like sandpaper, but the underside felt soft and smooth and spongy like a mushroom. I was afraid to touch them!

Diana volunteered to feed one, so the guide showed her how to hold her hand in a fist, let the fish stick up between her fingers, and let the stingray come up and take the fish. The stingray's mouth is a small square flap like a little trap door on its underside. Diana held her hand in a fist with the fish sticking up, and the stingray swam up and sucked it into the flap. I would never have done what Diana did! The stingrays were so big, my heart was beating really hard the whole time. It was amazing, and I was proud of myself for getting into the water. They did seem friendly.

Once we returned from swimming with the stingrays, we had just about an hour left before the tender took us back to the ship, so we talked Diana into going to the turtle farm. Several large tanks were there where turtles of different ages swam around, from little tiny turtles only a few inches long to the older turtles as big as a sandbox. We were allowed to pick up the little ones and hold them.

The researchers had developed a method of implanting white tissue from the turtles' lower shell onto the dark back of their shells so that they would be marked permanently, or tagged. That way, once the turtles were released, researchers could see if females with white spots were coming back to the Cayman Islands to lay their eggs. And researchers had recently documented that some had been coming back. That was so amazing the way the turtles found their way back to their birthplace.

Lauren videotaped me holding one of the little turtles, and it waved its front flippers in the air like it was trying to swim. Diana looked at the little turtle I was holding, and tears came to her eyes.

"Is that one of the turtles that will be released, or will it be eaten?" she said.

I was trying not to think about it.

"Time to head back to the boat," said Daddy, looking

at his watch. "We've packed in a lot today on Grand Cayman, haven't we?"

As we walked out onto the dock to catch the tender, I felt sunburned and tired. We had spent the whole day in the sun. We'd seen some beautiful and amazing animals. And Lauren and Diana hadn't fought all day! Was it too good to be true?

And what had Guy done today? I hoped I'd see him tonight.

9

DIANA

No more than thirty minutes after we got back on board, our ship left Grand Cayman. I went with Mom and Norm to stand on the upper deck to watch us pull away from the island. I could look out and see the lights of George Town begin to wink on, and Seven Mile Beach stretching away along the coastline as the sun set.

Lauren and Stephanie had gone back to take showers before dinner because they said they were sandy and sunburned. I needed a shower, too, but I didn't primp as much as they did, and I could take my turn last.

Mom and Norm came and stood next to me as I leaned against the railing watching the island slip away.

"We had a great day today, didn't we?" Mom said.

"Yeah."

"All the animals were really cool, weren't they?"

"Yeah. Getting to touch those stingrays was amazing." I was trying not to think about the turtles.

"How is everything going?" Mom asked. "Are you girls getting along okay?

"Yeah. Fine." I had already made the mistake of telling Grammy Verra about my argument with Lauren. She'd already told me I was wrong. I didn't want to hear it again from Mom or Norm.

"Okay, sweetie," Mom said, rubbing my shoulder. "I'm glad. If you need to talk about anything, let me know."

"That's right," Norm said. "There's a lot of togetherness on a trip like this, and it can sometimes be a challenge."

I wished Norm hadn't butted into the conversation. I wished I could just have had a couple of minutes with Mom. I wanted to ask her about the trip she made with Dad where she fed the iguana. Sometimes I thought about times they were together and having fun—like that trip to Saint Thomas—and I'd wonder what happened between them.

I shook my head, as if to shake the thoughts away. Deep down I knew that wasn't something I should spend my time thinking about. I knew it was right that they were apart and that Mom was with Norm.

I reminded myself that Norm had always tried to be nice to me. Not to replace my dad but to be a parent. He had even pulled me out of the Big Pigeon River two summers ago when I fell out of the raft. So I bit my tongue and didn't snap at Norm, and then I thought about how Dr. Shrink would say I was making progress.

The evening breeze blew a bit cooler.

"Better go get ready for dinner," Norm said.

So the three of us headed inside. Mom gave me a hug and a kiss on the forehead before they stepped into their room.

"See you in a little while, sweetie," she said.

Just as I was going into my room, I saw something move on the hallway floor, something with a tail, scurrying. It trundled around the corner into the supply room, where a lot of towels and soaps and shampoos were being stored.

I caught my breath. Goosebumps ran up the back of my neck. What was that?

I let the door close. I ran down the hall and peeked into the supply storage room, scanning the floor.

And as I leaned over a pile of folded towels, I saw a beautiful grayish-blue lizard. It was the cutest thing, with big bulging golden eyes with red rims and feet that looked like they had sucker cups on them. It stared at me, blinked, and then ran along the edge of the wall, behind another stack of towels.

I followed it.

What was a lizard doing on our cruise ship? Had it come from Grand Cayman? How did it get here?

Before it could run away, I tiptoed closer, knelt, and grabbed it. It struggled, but I held on to it and put it under my T-shirt, feeling its cool, dry skin and its feet scratching on my stomach; then I went into our room. Thankfully, Stephanie and Lauren had already taken their showers and left me a note. They had gone down to the teen club to meet Guy and Evan and shoot some videos before dinner. They said for me to come join them when I got ready. Fat chance of that now that I had a pet!

I took the lizard out from under my shirt and put it on my bed to look at it more closely. It was a mottled bluish-gray color, with eight V-shaped markings on its back from its head to its tail. It was about ten inches long, with those amazing golden eyes. Its feet were spindly and clawlike, and its tail was as thin as a strand of spaghetti. It looked up at me and blinked slowly. It looked like a little dragon or a little dinosaur! Its mouth curved around its jaw in a jaunty way, making it look like it had a cheeky smile on its face.

I thought about one of my favorite books when I was young, *Jeremy Thatcher, Dragon Hatcher* by Bruce Coville. He raised the dragon from an egg, keeping it a secret from everyone. He and the dragon dreamed the same dreams. Eventually he had to release the dragon because it grew too big. He was an artist, and the dragon, as it grew larger and larger, came to represent the power of his art. I had loved that book.

The lizard tried to run away, but I picked it up and put it on my palm. When I held out my finger, the lizard grasped it and crawled over my hand.

Where would I keep it? Carrying the lizard with me, I looked around the room and saw a shoebox. Inside was a pair of strappy sandals Stephanie had brought for our dress-up dinner. I took out the sandals and put them with her stuff, then used fingernail scissors to punch holes in the top of the box. I put the lizard in the bottom of the box and watched it. It sat and watched me with its golden eyes, then started trying to crawl out of the box. I hated to do it, but I put the top on.

Now what? What did it eat? Was this an iguana, like the one Mom described feeding on Saint Thomas when we were out on the beach today? If so, Mom had said the one she fed ate hibiscus flowers. I didn't know what else it ate. Were there some hibiscus flowers in pots in various places on deck? Maybe out by the pool. I wished I had grabbed hibiscus flowers from the island when I was there earlier today! If only I had known I'd need them! But I'd look around the ship for them.

I suddenly realized there was a lot I needed to find out about this lizard. There were computers in the teen club where I could look up stuff. Quickly I showered, and then I put my room key in my pocket. Before leaving, I checked on the iguana. He looked at me curiously. He was more gray now, less blue. I hated keeping him in the box, but right now I didn't know what else to do with him. I decided to name him Iggy, short for iguana.

"Bye, Iggy," I said. "You be good. Hopefully I'm going to be bringing you back something to eat."

I headed for the teen club. Stephanie and Lauren had already left, and a couple of kids were there that I hadn't seen before. Once in the computer room, I logged on and started surfing the Internet to find out about the lizard.

I found a YouTube video showing how to feed an iguana. Looking at the iguana on the video, I was almost sure that's what my lizard was. It looked like they would eat practically any vegetable, such as green beans, peppers, squash, okra, zucchini, carrots, or tomatoes. And any kind of greens, such as collard greens, kale, turnip greens, parsley, or spinach. They liked all kinds of melons, as well as bananas, grapes, and all kinds of berries. I was amazed at all the kinds of foods that iguanas could eat.

I could go to the buffet and get a lot of these things! We were supposed to eat at the restaurant tonight, but if I went to the buffet right now, I could sneak some food for him (or her—I had no idea whether Iggy was a boy or a girl).

I ran to the buffet and stood in line with my empty plate until I got to the salad bar and the vegetables. I put pieces of lettuce, watermelon, grapes, and canta-loupe on the plate. Then I went over to the vegetable bar and asked for kale, raw spinach, and green beans.

"What kind of meat?" asked the server.

"Oh, no meat," I said. "I've recently become a vegetarian."

The server smiled at me. "Good for you, very healthy," he said.

As soon as I got the kale, beans, and spinach, I acted like I was going out to the dining room, but then cut through and headed back for the elevator. As I stood in the elevator, a dressed-up woman looked at my plate and smiled.

"That's the way to keep your figure, honey," she said. "But you don't look like you need to watch your weight."

"Oh, I know!" I said in a very friendly way. "I'm just trying to eat healthy, that's all."

"Good for you."

Once I got off on my floor, I peeked through the doorway down the hall and then ran as fast as I could with the plate, digging my key card out of my pocket as I went. I didn't want to run into Mom or Norm in the hall. And I had no idea what I would tell Stephanie and Lauren. For now, I just wanted to keep this a secret. Just like Jeremy had in the book.

I swiped my key card, then went into my room lightning fast, letting the door slam behind me. I put the plate up on my bunk and then climbed up with the box. I opened the top, and there was Iggy, blinking at me with his golden eyes and his enigmatic smile, as quiet as he could be. I picked out a piece of raw spinach, broke it into a couple of bite-size pieces, and offered it to him, letting the edge of the spinach touch his mouth. Very slowly, he reached out his neck and gave the spinach a flick of his tongue. He brought his tongue back into his mouth for a second or two, then flicked his tongue at the spinach again. Finally, he reached out and bit down on the spinach, and equally slowly, he began to chew.

He was eating it! He was so cute, I couldn't believe it.

"Good job, Iggy. Are you hungry? What kind of scary journey did you have today? Did you come here from Grand Cayman?"

His amber eyes regarded me serenely, and he finished the piece of spinach. As he was eating, his skin seemed to turn a brighter color of blue. Or was it my imagination? I had a crazy idea to tell Mom about feeding Iggy the spinach, since she'd fed the hibiscus flower to the iguana in Saint Thomas.

I was glad I had the upper bunk. I could keep Iggy up here in his box and even put the food in the corner of my bunk and lay a couple of blankets over them. Lauren and Stephanie might never notice.

Just then I heard Lauren and Stephanie talking out in the hall. I dropped the rest of the spinach in the box and slammed the top back on it, then pushed the box back in the corner of my bed under the covers.

The door opened, and Lauren and Stephanie came in.

"Hey! We were at the teen club. Did you see our note?" Stephanie said. "We were looking for you."

"I went to the teen club, but I didn't see you," I said. "Did you guys leave?" I glanced at the box at the end of my bed. Did I hear scratching?

"Yeah," said Lauren, "we left for a little while. We went out on deck to videotape some stuff."

"After dinner we're going to go down to the employee section of the ship and videotape. You can come with us," Stephanie said.

"That's okay." I didn't want to leave Iggy. I wanted to let him crawl around on my bed.

"Come on, we want you to come," she insisted.

There was a knock on our door. "Girls, time for dinner" came Norm's voice. "We're heading for the restaurant!"

I put my book on top of the box to keep the lid on before I climbed down from my bunk.

Dinner was nerve-racking. I couldn't stop thinking about Iggy. Grammy Verra asked me questions about my day on Grand Cayman, and I could hardly answer.

After dinner, Lauren and Stephanie wanted me to come to the teen club with them, and I didn't want them to get too suspicious, so I said I'd go. Plus I wanted to read more about iguanas.

"Let's ask Josh if we can interview him," Lauren said as we got off the elevator outside the teen club. "Then maybe we can look around for Manuel's room and see if there's anything suspicious about it."

"Let's just forget all about that," Stephanie said.

"Yeah, I probably imagined it," I said. "I vote we forget about it too."

"No!" Lauren said. "It's intriguing."

Guy and Evan were already at the teen club and came over to us the minute we came in. They were both wearing new Grand Cayman T-shirts. Guy was talking mainly to Stephanie, tossing his brown hair out of his eyes in that annoying way he had, and Evan, skinny and nervous, was talking mainly to Lauren. They kind of ignored me. I didn't care. I had a dragon back in the room.

"Hey, what did you guys do on Grand Cayman today?" Evan asked. "Our two families went scuba diving at a coral reef and saw a barracuda!"

"Oh gosh, were you scared?" Stephanie asked. "I thought I saw a barracuda when I was snorkeling, but it was just a needlefish."

"No, I wasn't scared. They don't attack in clear water," Evan said in a superior voice. "We weren't worried."

Boys were always bragging. Give me a break.

While they were talking, I went over to the computers and looked up iguanas again. There were some YouTubes on caring for a pet iguana, and I watched one that explained that because an iguana was a reptile, its body wasn't able to warm itself, and it needed to sit in the sun or under a heat lamp each day.

Oh no! How was I going to let the iguana sit out in

the sun without someone seeing us? I kind of panicked over that, trying to figure out what I might be able to get away with. Somebody was bound to see me.

Stephanie came over, and I quickly exited out of the YouTube screen and pretended to be looking at music videos.

"What's up?" I asked.

"We're going to try to go down to the employee part of the ship and shoot some video. Are you coming with us?"

I didn't want to be away from Iggy any longer. "No, I think I'll head back to the room. I have a horse book that I've been wanting to read."

Back in the room alone, I quickly checked on Iggy and gave him some green beans and kale. He didn't seem to like the beans as much as the spinach, but he flicked his tongue at them just like before and then slowly chewed them up. He really liked the kale. Then I put him out on top of my bed. He wanted to walk all over my comforter. His walk was kind of like a sashay, with his hips moving back and forth to balance the movement of his tail. I tried rubbing him under the chin the way one person had done in the videos I'd watched, and he did seem to like it. He still seemed to have that funny little smile on his face.

Who would have ever thought that I'd have a baby iguana as a pet on a cruise ship? All this time I'd been worrying about trying not to fight with Lauren and trying to get along with Stephanie, but now none of that mattered at all, because I had my very own little dragon to care for on the rest of the cruise.

At the same time, I was wondering, *How in the world did he get on the ship?* Someone would have had to bring him on board. But why?

10

STEPHANIE

I didn't know what was going on with Diana. She acted so jealous of Lauren and me at first, and then she started acting like she didn't care what we did.

I had been trying to include her with what we were doing. Like, I asked her several times to come down to the employee part of the ship with us to videotape. She wasn't interested.

When Lauren and I first went through the door that said Employees Only, I did feel strange, like we were doing something we shouldn't be doing. But Lauren just went straight through without hesitating. We walked down the hall, by all the closed doors. Daddy had said there were almost as many staff on the ship as there were guests, so there were a lot of employee rooms.

We peeked into a bar, with bottles lining a mirrored wall behind the counter, which was just for employees. Lauren was going to shoot some video, but there was hardly anyone in there, so she changed her mind.

Then we found the employee cafeteria, or mess hall, and a lot of people were in there eating dinner. It wasn't as nicely decorated as the parts of the ship that were for customers. The tables were long rectangles, in tight rows. Most of the employees were still in their uniforms. We even saw Manuel eating dinner, and Lauren started videotaping him while he was having a conversation with the guy across the table from him. Manuel didn't see us at first; he and the other guy were leaning in, and their conversation was pretty intense.

Suddenly Manuel shook his head, and then he glanced up and saw us. A look of anger came across his face, and he wasn't as friendly and polite as he had been when we interviewed him in our room. "What are you girls doing here in the employee cafeteria?"

"We're just working on that project for school," Lauren said, taking the camera away from her eye and holding it close against her body, "and we're videotaping in different places on the ship."

"Did you ask the cruise director if you were allowed to come down here?"

"No," Lauren said. "We didn't think there would be anything wrong with it."

"Sorry," I said. I felt terrible!

"You should get permission before coming down here," said the guy sitting with Manuel, who looked and sounded American. I wondered if it was the American roommate he'd told us about.

Manuel put down his napkin and stood up. "Let me walk you young ladies out." He herded us out of the cafeteria and down the hall. "The management is very strict about who is allowed down here," he said in an apologetic tone. "If you ask the cruise director, and he says yes you can come, then that would be okay."

"We just want to know what goes on behind the scenes," said Lauren.

"Go see the cruise director and see what he says." Manuel held the Employees Only door ajar for us. "Bye, girls," he said. "See you later!"

We stood in the hallway outside the door.

"We should have asked before going in there," I said. "I hope we're not in trouble."

"Dad says it's better to ask forgiveness than to ask

permission. I'm glad we went! And we can ask the cruise director. Manuel sure seemed anxious to get rid of us, though, didn't he?"

We headed down the long hall and then took the elevator back up to the teen-club deck. Back in the teen club, Guy and Evan stopped playing video games long enough to ask about the video we'd shot in the employee section of the boat.

"Oh, we just took a short little piece," I said. "They told us we had to leave."

"Can we see it?" asked Guy.

Lauren shrugged. "Sure, let's watch it." Lauren plugged the camera into one of the video monitors near the editing suite.

We saw her wide shot of the employee cafeteria, with the plain linoleum tables lined up. Then we saw the camera pan across the various people in uniform eating at the tables and focus on Manuel and the guy with the American accent talking.

"Turn it up," said Evan. "See if you can hear what they're saying."

Lauren turned up the video, and we watched.

Manuel said, "It is gone, that is all."

The American said, "What do you mean, it's gone? How did it get away?"

"I do not know," said Manuel.

"You have to find it," said the American.

"I have looked. I cannot find it anywhere." Then Manuel shook his head, looked up, and saw us. He asked us what we were doing there.

Lauren paused the tape. "So, that's their conversation."

"I wonder what's gone?" I said curiously.

"Yeah, rerun it," said Guy.

We watched the scene again, then sat quietly, thinking.

"So something has gotten away, and the American told Manuel that he had to find it," said Lauren. "I wonder what it is. I wonder if it's connected to what Diana heard them talking about before."

"What's that?" asked Evan.

"Diana overheard them talking about doing something illegal," said Lauren.

"Whoa," said Guy. "Weird."

"I don't like talking about this," I said. "Manuel is so nice. And he has all those little children at home in the Philippines."

"Yeah, but something is definitely weird," Lauren said.

"Let's just have fun on our vacation and forget about this, Lauren," I said. "I don't want to think about it. Grammy's birthday celebration is tomorrow, at the dress-up dinner, and we have to make plans for that. I want us to write speeches or maybe a poem for Grammy."

"That's so like you, Stephanie, wanting everything to always be so perfect," she said. "Well, sometimes things just aren't."

"All you have to do is ask the cruise director. He'll probably say yes, and then you'll be able to investigate," Guy said.

"Meanwhile we can keep an eye on Manuel when he comes to straighten our room," Lauren said.

Josh came over to us. "What's up, guys? Your faces look like trouble."

"Do you think we could get permission to videotape down in the employee part of the ship?" I asked.

"What for?"

"We just want to see what goes on behind the scenes," Lauren said. "It's for a school project, since we're missing a few days of school to come on this trip."

"My first thought is the answer would be no," Josh said. "They're pretty strict about guests not going into the employee area. But I suppose I could ask the cruise director."

"That would be great," said Lauren.

As soon as Josh left, Evan said, "Hey, it's almost time for *Pirates of the Caribbean* to start on the outdoor screen. Should we go?"

"Yeah!" Guy said.

We checked with the 'rents, and they said it was okay, so we took the elevator to the top deck and headed out under the stars. The staff had arranged all the lounge chairs in rows for watching the movie on the big screen. Warm blankets were neatly folded on each lounge chair. A lot of people were already out here, and waiters were bringing drinks and snacks for the movie.

"Ooh, this looks comfy!" Lauren said. She climbed onto a chair and spread a blanket over her legs.

We were only able to find three lounge chairs together.

"Well ... two of us could share, I guess," Lauren said. "Come on, Stephanie, you and I can share."

"Okay!" Giggling, I crawled under the blanket with Lauren.

Guy took the chair on my side, and Evan took the chair on Lauren's side. We scooted the three chairs close together so they touched.

It was a beautiful night, and brilliant stars were spread out over us. The water all around us made a hushed noise, and the boat's engines purred beneath us.

All of us had already seen the movie when it first came out, but we were always up for watching *Pirates of the Caribbean* again. In this one, Jack Sparrow was searching for the Fountain of Youth, but so were Blackbeard and his daughter.

"I can't wait to see the part about the mermaids again," I told Guy. "I've always loved mermaids."

"These aren't good mermaids, though," Guy said.

"Well, one is," I said.

"I wish I could order something from one of those waiters," Evan said. "I think it's so cool to sit out here and order something. You just charge it to your room, right?"

"Yeah," Lauren said. "Hey, check out those people making out over there."

We all looked over at two people not far away sharing a lounge chair. They were wrapped around each other under the blanket, their faces close together in the dark.

"Oooh," said Evan. He made a kissing noise.

"Evan!" said Lauren. "Be quiet!" But she giggled.

I curled both arms underneath the blanket. As I watched the movie, I was aware of Lauren snuggled next to me on the lounge chair. I was even more aware of Guy next to me on the other side. The evening air was cool, and he was warmer than Lauren, and fidgeted less.

There was one scene in the movie where a scary mermaid popped out of the water next to a boat, and I screamed and put my hands over my mouth. As I took my hand away, Guy reached over and took it. I was surprised at first, but I didn't pull away. His hand was warm. I could feel my heart beating and could hardly pay attention to the rest of the movie. I let my hand remain in his, where all my nerve endings were at full alert and my whole arm began to tingle.

Once the movie was over, Lauren wanted to wander around and videotape some more. Evan said he'd go with her.

"Want to just stay here and look at the stars for a few minutes?" Guy asked me.

"Sure." My mouth felt dry, and my heart thudded, but I wanted to.

"Okay, so you guys are staying here?" Lauren said carefully.

"Yeah, just for a few minutes. We'll meet you back at the teen club," I said, ignoring the look she gave me.

As soon as Lauren and Evan were gone, a silence fell over us. I couldn't think of a thing to say. At the same time, I was acutely aware of Guy sitting right next to me. My mind raced through a dozen thoughts as I scanned the star-spangled sky, and my heart began to beat faster.

"So, what's with your stepsister, Diana?" he asked. "She isn't hanging out with us much anymore."

"I don't know. She's definitely been acting a little different," I said. "But she isn't much for groups." I didn't want to say anything negative about Diana.

"I get that. I don't like big groups that much either. Because of my diabetes, I've always felt a little different. People watch me when I test myself and bolus and ask a bunch of questions, and sometimes it feels awkward."

"Bolus? What's that? Now I'm asking questions."

"That's okay. That's when I give myself a dose of insulin to correct my blood sugar. But anyway, having diabetes has helped me understand what it's like for people who might be different. And sometimes people can be mean."

"Are people mean to you?"

"Sometimes." He turned on his side and snared me with a challenging look. "Once in a soccer game, the coach put me in, and another guy on the team said, 'I can't believe you're putting *him* in!' like I was the worst player on the team or something. I know it was because I have to be careful about my blood sugar when I'm exercising, and I have to sip Gatorade through practice. That hurt. Anyway, are people mean to Diana?"

"Yeah. Some kids call her 'annn-i-mal' in the hallway at school."

"Where'd that come from?"

I hesitated. I hadn't told anyone about this. "I think it came from me."

"You're kidding. You said something mean about Diana? I thought you were close."

I sat up to explain. I wanted him to see that I hadn't meant it. "I told someone once, when I was mad at Diana, that she liked animals better than people. And then I guess that girl told some other people, and some kids started calling her 'annn-i-mal.' I didn't mean to start it. I didn't mean anything by it. I didn't know the girl would repeat what I said."

"What does Diana think about it?"

"Oh, it really hurts her feelings when people say that. But she doesn't know that it was me that started it."

"You have to tell her and say you're sorry," Guy said.

I didn't say anything. I knew he was right.

"You have to take responsibility for what you did," he added.

"But do you think she'll forgive me?"

Guy regarded me seriously. "Maybe not right away."

"I don't know if I can do that. She'll get so mad."

Guy was silent for a few minutes. He seemed to be thinking about saying something and then changed his mind. He looked up at the sky. "The stars are so bright out here on the ocean."

I knew he was thinking that I wasn't brave enough to tell Diana. And maybe that's what it took. Bravery.

He raised up on his elbow and pushed my hair back from my forehead. Then he reached for my hand again.

I could feel myself blushing. Something was about to happen.

It was as if the ship stopped there in the middle of the ocean and the earth stopped turning.

And then he leaned down and very lightly pressed his lips onto mine for a moment. His lips were very soft and warm. He pulled away, and I could hear him breathe, then he touched his lips to mine again. Mine tingled for a long moment after his lips were gone. His breath smelled like peppermint gum.

My first kiss! Under the stars in the middle of the ocean!

"Hey!" Suddenly Lauren was right up in our faces, running the video camera. "I got it! I got it on camera!"

Gasping, Guy and I jerked apart from each other. "Lauren!"

"You knew I wasn't going to leave you alone for too long," Lauren said, laughing. Guy and I both sat up, embarrassed. "Besides, it's almost curfew. We have to go back to the room."

All in a rush, before I even knew what was happening, I was saying good night to Guy. He lightly touched my elbow as he moved away.

"I can't believe you did that!" I told Lauren as we headed down to our deck on the elevator.

"Well, I didn't want you to get in trouble by being late for curfew."

"Still, you didn't have to videotape us!"

"It was just a joke!"

"Well, I don't think it's very funny, Lauren!"

"Well, I mean, did you have anything to hide?"

"No!" I said, confused. "But whether we had anything to hide or not, you didn't need to videotape us."

We headed back to the room in silence. My heart was beating hard, and I could feel the heat of anger on my face. I hadn't ever really fought with Lauren before.

When we got back to the room, Diana was in bed reading.

"Did y'all have fun?" she asked. She didn't even seem that curious about what we'd done.

"Yeah, it was pretty exciting, actually," Lauren said as she stretched out on her bed. "You missed out."

It made me mad that Lauren was trying to make Diana feel like she missed a lot.

"You didn't miss that much," I said. "We just went down to the employee cafeteria and videotaped a little bit and kind of got in trouble, that's all. And then we watched the movie under the stars."

"You got in trouble?" Diana said, her chin on her hands on the edge of her bunk.

"Yeah, a little." I told her about what had happened, and about the conversation we'd taped.

She listened and nodded her head thoughtfully. "So

Manuel is supposed to find something that they've lost. I wonder what that is."

"I have no idea," I said. "But it's alive, because he said, 'It got away.'"

Diana nodded her head again, thoughtfully. She had a funny expression on her face, as if she was thinking about something. But she didn't say anything.

"Anyway, listen, why don't we write a speech or a song for Grammy's birthday celebration? Or maybe a poem?" I asked. "It's tomorrow night, so we only have tonight and tomorrow during the day. I'd love to see her face if we write a song."

"We could videotape ourselves singing "Happy Birthday" or reciting a poem we've written," Lauren said.

"Why is everything about videotaping for you?" Diana said irritably. "That seems like all you think about."

Lauren sat up straight on her bed and made a face. "Well, I'm sorry; it's fun!"

"Why can't we talk about something else?" Diana added.

"Well, that's kind of rude," said Lauren.

My heart started beating harder, and I could feel my chest getting tight. Uh-oh. This was turning into another argument. At the same time, I'd had about enough of Lauren's video camera myself. I couldn't believe she taped Guy and me. What if she decided to show it to Daddy?

"Let's talk about Grammy's birthday. We could just sing a song or recite a poem in person at dinner," I said. "She might really appreciate that. What about singing an ode to Jelly, her dog? She's so crazy about her dog. She'd like that!"

Both Lauren and Diana sat on their bunks sulking. Neither of them answered. I searched around in my mind for something else to talk about that wouldn't cause drama.

"Let's show each other what we're wearing for Grammy's birthday tomorrow night. It's dress-up night." I reached into the tiny closet and held out the sleeveless yellow sundress I was planning to wear. I knew the color looked good with my dark hair. "This is what I'm wearing," I said. "What do you guys think? And my new sandals." I saw my strappy silver heels standing on the floor of the closet, but I didn't see the shoebox they came in. "That's funny. Where's my shoebox? Did anybody see it?"

"No," Diana said.

"I haven't seen it," Lauren said.

"Well, it's not that big a deal, but I was pretty sure I brought my sandals in that shoebox." I looked through the rest of the things in the closet and then under my bed and Lauren's bed. "Just kind of weird, that's all."

"Maybe you took them out of the box to pack them and then just forgot about it," Lauren said.

"Maybe." But I was pretty sure I had packed them in the box. I'd been afraid they'd get crushed, since they were new. I looked under the beds again but didn't find the box. Diana lay on the bunk above me in her pj's, with the covers piled up around her feet, reading her horse book. "Oh, well. Anyway, what are you wearing tomorrow, Lauren?"

"I have a couple of dressy dresses, because a lot of people in my class had bar and bat mitzvahs this past year," Lauren said. "I brought two to pick from. There's this one that I told you about—royal blue off the shoulder, and the other's a strapless black-and-white print with a little jacket with capped sleeves. I'll make up my mind tomorrow when I'm getting dressed."

I didn't need to ask Diana what she was wearing. I had gone with Lynn to get a dress for Diana one day when she was at the barn, because she had refused to go. Lynn and I have fun shopping together. She and I had tried to pick out a dress we thought Diana might like. We knew she didn't like bright colors or frilly styles, so we found her a deep purple empire waist with spaghetti straps and just a few ruffles, not many, on the top. I don't even know if she tried it on before bringing it. It was hanging in our small closet here on the ship.

"Diana is wearing this," I said, showing the dress to Lauren. "Lynn and I picked it out for her. Don't you like it?"

"Sure," said Lauren noncommittally. She was playing with her camera, not looking at the dress.

"You like it, right, Diana?"

"Sure," she said after a second, turning a page in her book.

I put the dress away and got ready for bed, listening to the awkward silence in the room. I started to get mad. Diana was always picking fights with people and Lauren wouldn't stop videotaping everything, and here we were on this great trip and I was having to try to keep the peace. Not that I was perfect or anything. But I decided to stop trying so hard to make conversation. They were going to have to do some of it themselves. I got out my book and climbed into my bunk, below Diana.

I started trying to read but still felt mad. Why was Diana like this? Why was I always in the middle with her and someone else? When we'd gone to the Outer Banks, she'd gotten mad at Cody, the boy we met there, because he'd made a mistake. It was a big mistake, granted, but it was still a mistake. She picked fights, and she didn't forgive people for things they did.

I had given her a lecture on forgiving people, because

I think that we all make mistakes sometimes. None of us are perfect. The only one who is perfect is God.

While I was sitting there thinking, I heard a scratching noise coming from Diana's bunk.

"What's that noise?" I said.

"What noise?" Diana said.

"That scratching noise."

"I don't hear anything."

"How can you not hear anything? I hear a scratching noise." I got up, climbed up on her bunk, and pulled back the blanket.

"Hey, stop it!" Diana yelled.

But not before I saw my shoebox sitting up there in the back corner of her bunk.

"What's my shoebox doing up here? And why does it have holes cut in the top?"

11

DIANA

I tried to keep Stephanie from taking off the box top, but she reached out and flipped the top off, before I could stop her. Iggy poked his head over the edge, with his funny smile.

And Stephanie screamed.

I knew she would.

"What is that?" she yelled.

"What is what?" Lauren jumped up from her bunk, videotaping everything that happened, which made me so mad, I wanted to break the camera.

"It's Iggy. An iguana," I said. "He won't hurt you." I felt a sudden stab of sadness that they had found out about him, and he wasn't just my secret alone.

"Oh my gosh, I can't believe you're keeping a lizard in our room!" Stephanie sat down on her bunk, with her palm flat over her breastbone, taking deep breaths. "Where did you get it?"

There was a knock on our door, and Luke, wearing his pj's, poked his head in. "Mom and Dad said they heard a scream and wanted to know if everything was all right," he said.

"Everything is fine," I said, my heart pounding, as I quickly covered the box with the end of my blanket. "We're just fooling around, having fun. It was a fun scream, not a scared scream."

Stephanie glanced at me, opened her mouth, and then closed it. She looked at Luke and smiled. "I was the one who screamed," she said. "I'm sorry."

Luke cocked his head and stared at us. He saw Lauren sitting there filming the whole time. He made a fish face at the camera, then crossed his eyes, then uncrossed them.

"Sure?"

"Sure," I said.

"Is my sister with her camera driving you crazy?"

"Yes."

"Okay," he said, and then shut the door.

Stephanie took a deep breath. "What is that, and where did you get it, Diana?"

I opened the box and took Iggy out, holding him out to her. His skin felt dry and cool, and I worried about him getting enough sun. "It's an iguana," I said, "and I found him in the supply room just off the hallway beside our room. I saw him wandering down the hall."

Stephanie shrank away. "Does it bite?"

"No, he's gentle."

"You found an iguana wandering down the hall outside our room?" Lauren asked.

"I'm not going to answer any questions while you've got that camera on," I said.

Lauren put the camera down. "Okay. It's off."

So I told them how I found the iguana, and how I had looked up iguanas online in the teen club and had been feeding Iggy from the buffet.

"I want to see you feed it," Lauren said. "Can I video-tape you feeding it?"

"Okay, watch." I picked up a small leaf of kale from the plate of vegetables I had wedged at the foot of my bed and offered it to Iggy. "First he'll flick it with his tongue."

Sure enough, Iggy gave the kale two rapid flicks before taking the leaf and chewing on it.

"Aww! He's cute," Lauren said.

"I know. He's like a little dragon or dinosaur, isn't he?" I said.

"A lizard is cute?" Stephanie said. "I can't believe you said that. What are you going to do with it? You can't keep it at the foot of your bed for the rest of our trip. I'm afraid he'll get away and be crawling on me at night or something. And what about when we go home? Are you going to take it home with you?"

"I don't know," I admitted. "I haven't thought about any of those things." I'd just been trying to figure out things as I went.

"Why would an iguana be walking down the hallway outside our room?" Stephanie asked.

"Maybe someone brought it onto the ship, and it escaped from them," Lauren said. "Maybe that's what Manuel and his American friend are looking for."

There was silence in our room for a minute as we all thought about what she'd suggested.

"A lost iguana? Why would they bring an iguana on the ship? And why would it be a big deal?" I asked. Then it occurred to me: they were endangered. "Remember when we were on Grand Cayman, Mom was reading to us about some of the endangered animals on the island? The blue iguana is an endangered type of iguana. I wonder if this is a blue iguana." I was letting him walk across my bedspread now.

"He doesn't look blue. He looks gray," said Lauren.

"Sometimes he looks more blue than this. Maybe they change colors for some reason," I said. "Tomorrow I can go back to the teen club and look up blue iguanas to see if I can find a picture of a young one."

"So what if he is a blue iguana? Do you think he would be worth a lot of money?" Lauren asked.

"I don't know," I said. "Maybe."

"I don't think I'm going to be able to sleep with that lizard in our room tonight," Stephanie said. "I'll keep dreaming that it's going to walk across my face or something."

"You can't be scared of this little thing," I said.

"You could get in trouble for hiding it, Diana. I think we should tell Daddy and Lynn about it."

"I didn't do anything wrong. All I did was find and feed him," I told her. Stephanie was always such a scaredy-cat. She was always worried about doing something wrong.

"If Manuel and his friend brought the iguana on the ship, maybe they're smuggling it," Lauren said. "Maybe that's what they were talking about when Manuel said what they were doing is illegal. Maybe it's a crime to smuggle an endangered animal."

"And maybe *you're* smuggling by hiding it," Stephanie said.

"Tomorrow I'll find out what kind of crime it is to smuggle an iguana, and if anyone would ever even do that. Meanwhile, all I'm doing is taking care of an animal I found." I stared Stephanie down. "You aren't going to tell on me, are you?"

Stephanie stood by the bed and looked down at her feet. "I think we should tell Daddy and Lynn. But I won't tell them. I'll let you do it."

"And what if they ask you about it?"

"I can't lie about it, Diana. I'm sorry." She looked at me wide-eyed, but with her jaw set.

"I think we should try to find out if this is what Manuel and the other guy are looking for. If we could somehow videotape them in their cabin, we might be able to tape a conversation just like we did in the cafeteria. We might find out a lot," said Lauren.

"Well, we can't find out about that until tomorrow when Josh asks," I said. "Let's just go to sleep."

"I don't think we should wait for Josh to ask," Lauren said. "I think we should just do it."

I put Iggy back in his box, and Lauren went over and turned out the light.

"You better not let him out during the night," Stephanie said as she climbed under her covers.

The next morning Iggy was the first thing I thought about when I woke up. I sat up and opened his box, then put him out on the bedspread to walk around. He was still mostly gray today. I was starting to feel bad about keeping him in a box, and now that Lauren and Stephanie knew about him, I didn't have to keep him cooped up anymore. I could let him walk all over the room. I didn't want him to fall off my bunk, though!

Maybe I could keep him in the shower.

I created mountain ranges with my covers and let him crawl over them. He found a perch on one of my legs, and I scratched him under the chin. He held his head up at just the right angle. When I held my finger in front of him, he would grasp it and hold on, and I could pick him up and let him hang from his front legs. Then I fed him the last of the kale and beans, which he took right out of my hand and chewed slowly, staring at me with his golden eyes. I would have to go back to the buffet today to get him more food.

When Lauren and Stephanie woke up, they wanted to come to the teen club with me to do more research on blue iguanas. We quickly got dressed and ready to go.

"What do you think?" I asked. "Should I leave him in the shower and shut the shower door? That would leave him a few feet to walk around in, and I could put his plate of food there too."

"But then we'll have to take a shower in there!" Stephanie squealed.

For once, Lauren and I agreed and out voted Stephanie. And we decided to leave the Do Not Disturb sign on our door so Manuel wouldn't come in and see him.

On the computer at the teen club, before even getting breakfast, we quickly found out about blue iguanas. The only place in the world they inhabited was Grand Cayman. They were the rarest iguanas in the world, magnificent dragon-like, dusky-blue creatures that could grow to over five feet long and live to be eighty years old. But hatchlings were small, like Iggy, only eight to ten inches long, and the biggest threats to them were snakes. It was illegal to keep blue iguanas as pets. Fights between male iguanas over females and territory could be extremely violent.

A few years ago, because of destruction of their habitat and being preyed upon by feral cats and dogs, there were so few blue iguanas living in the wild that they were considered extinct. An organization called BIRP, or the Blue Iguana Recovery Programme, was started on Grand Cayman in 1990. Scientists began breeding the iguanas in captivity and then releasing them into the wild to try to restore the blue iguana population. The program had been a tremendous success, and by 2010 there were six hundred fifty blue iguanas. The goal of the program was to increase the size of the blue iguana population to one thousand, and to set aside enough habitat on Grand Cayman for them to live comfortably in the wild.

"Iggy is one of the rarest iguanas in the world!" I said to Stephanie and Lauren. "Isn't that cool?"

"And that's amazing that he could live to be eighty years old," Lauren said, leaning over the console to see my computer screen. "He could live to be older than Grammy! Hey, how about if we make a video about Iggy's life on the cruise ship? We can show him hanging around in our room, and you going to the buffet to get him food."

"But it's illegal to keep an iguana like this as a pet," Stephanie said. "What we're doing is wrong. It's a wild animal. A very rare wild animal."

What Stephanie was saying made sense, but I didn't want to hear it. "But he's like my little dragon!" I said. "I found him!"

"If some expert were telling you this stuff, you'd listen to them, Diana," Stephanie said. "You're not listening because it's me saying this to you."

I thought about what Stephanie had just said. It was true that on the website it did say that it was illegal to keep a blue iguana as a pet. And his color hadn't been bright since I'd had him. I wondered if they turned gray when they were scared or unhappy. With the wild horses last spring, Stephanie and I had encountered a situation where the animals needed to survive without human interference. A volunteer who had many years' experience working with the wild horses had convinced me not to try to feed them. Maybe this little iguana was the same.

I took a deep breath. Much as I hated to admit it, Stephanie was probably right. "Okay," I said. "Until after Grammy's birthday celebration. Then I'll tell Mom and Norm about it."

"So that's our deal? You'll tell them after Grammy's birthday?"

"Yes, I promise."

"Look at this," said Lauren, who had been reading the website while Stephanie and I had been talking. "It says on here that the blue iguanas need sunlight to live. They have to physically sit in the sun every day. How are we going to do that? We need to somehow take him out on deck."

"I knew about that," I said "I read something about it before. We have to figure out how to do that." Maybe the iguana would turn blue with a little sun. I couldn't help but think that somehow I wasn't taking the right care of Iggy, and that's why he wasn't bright blue.

"Well, that's impossible. People will see him," Stephanie said.

"Maybe we can somehow hide him," I said. I didn't know how, but I'd figure it out.

12

STEPHANIE

We left the teen club and went to the buffet. We decided we'd get breakfast, and then Diana would go back and get food for Iggy.

While we were finishing our breakfast, Evan and Guy came over with their trays and sat at our table. I was dying to tell the boys about Iggy, but I knew it was important to keep it a secret.

"Morning!" said Guy, putting his tray next to mine. I tried to catch his eye, to see if he acted any different since last night, and he did glance at me more often. While Guy had a normal amount of food on his tray, Evan had waffles, an omelette, cantaloupe, two kinds of sausage, a blueberry muffin, grits, and cereal.

"Look at all that food!" I teased Evan. "You're a pig!"

"One of the greatest things about being on a cruise," Evan said.

"How do you stay so skinny?" Lauren asked him.

"I guess I just use up a lot of energy," Evan said, pouring syrup on his waffles.

I noticed Guy hadn't started eating yet. Instead, he had his insulin pump and meter in his lap. He inserted a test strip into his meter, and then pricked his index finger and squeezed a tiny drop of blood from his finger onto the test strip. A number appeared on the meter.

"Is that your blood glucose level?" I asked.

"Yeah." He typed the number showing on the meter into the pump.

"You're telling the pump what your blood glucose level is?"

"Yep. Then I enter the carbs in the meal that I'm about to eat. Let's see … I have scrambled eggs, which are excellent if you're counting carbs, because they're almost nothing, but I'll count them as one; bacon, which is about one carb; cantaloupe, which is about three; a Danish, which is about thirty carbs; and a glass of milk, which is about twelve. See, it tests your math skills. That adds up to forty-seven, so I input that into the pump, and then it translates that to insulin units and pumps it into me."

"That's pretty cool," I said.

"Much cooler than having to stick myself to inject the insulin. It doesn't hurt at all."

"How do you know how many carbs each food has? Do you memorize it?"

"I used a booklet at first, but yeah, now I kind of know the foods I eat most often by heart. If I have to look something up I can use my phone and go online."

"And you have to watch what you eat, right?" I said to Guy.

"Well, yeah, but I can bolus if I want to splurge on something like waffles."

"Cool," said Lauren. Then, suddenly, she said, "Guess what?"

Diana and I quickly looked at her. What was she doing? Was she going to tell about Iggy?

"What?" Evan said, taking a bite of his waffle.

"We found a wild iguana," Lauren whispered. "We're keeping it in our room."

I let my mouth drop open, and I stared at Diana, who glared at Lauren.

"Lauren!" Diana said with fury in her voice.

"Whoa, really?" Evan said. "You're kidding. Where'd you find it? Did you bring it from Grand Cayman? I heard they had a park there where they're breeding them and releasing them into the wild."

"I want to see it!" Guy said excitedly, tossing his hair back.

"What do you think you're doing, Lauren?" Diana said.

Lauren shrugged. "They already know about the thing that Manuel and his American friend lost. I just thought I'd bring them up to speed."

"But I thought it was obvious that we were going to keep it a secret!" Diana said.

"I thought that just meant the 'rents," Lauren said. "I didn't know you didn't want to tell the guys either."

"Well, we know now," Guy said. "So can we come see it after breakfast?"

"Sure," said Lauren.

Diana stood up and threw her fork down on her plate, narrowing her eyes at Lauren. "I cannot believe you told them about it! What's the matter with you?" She marched away from the table.

Oh no! I couldn't figure out why Lauren decided to tell the boys, either. We hadn't talked about it at all. And I didn't know if Daddy and Lynn would think it was okay for the guys to come to our room. I was staring at Lauren with my mouth open when the captain made an announcement. "Attention please. Today we will spend the day at sea. The weather is a balmy eighty degrees with scattered clouds. We will be heading northwest at eighteen knots with a light wind. Please enjoy all of our shipboard amenities." The captain went on to describe a cooking class, an art show, and a yoga class that would be taking place today on the ship.

I noticed Diana over by the buffet getting food for Iggy, and I went over to talk to her.

"I'm sorry that Lauren told," I said. "I have no idea why she did it!"

"What is wrong with her? Every five minutes she does something to make me mad!" Diana said. "I'm going back to the room. And don't bring the guys to see Iggy. He's a wild animal, and he might freak out with all of us in there."

A minute later she left with a plate of veggies and fruits.

I headed back to the table and slid into my seat. "She's really mad, Lauren. She doesn't want us to bring the boys back to the room."

Lauren tossed her head. "Well, there's nothing I can do now. They already know. We might as well show it to them."

"We won't tell anyone," Guy said reassuringly. "We promise."

"It's just the principle of the thing," I said. I didn't want to leave the group, but I felt like I needed to try to talk to Diana. "I think I'll go now too."

"Where are you going?" Guy said as soon as I stood up. He was looking at me in a way that made me feel confused and flustered.

"Back to the room."

"Can we come see the iguana?" he asked.

"Let me go talk to Diana first. She's pretty upset."

When I got back, Diana had Iggy in the middle of the room, letting him eat from the plate of greens she'd brought him.

"He's supposed to be a secret!" she exclaimed the minute I walked in. "Maybe those guys will tell their parents, and pretty soon all kinds of people are going to know about him."

I sat down beside her. "Lauren was wrong to tell the guys about it, I agree with you. She should not have done that. But I think we need to go ahead and tell Daddy and Lynn about this. We could get in serious trouble by keeping this iguana. We might be committing a crime! We should turn it in."

"I promised I'd tell them after Grammy's birthday tonight. So that's when I'll tell them," Diana said.

"We might as well let the boys see him," I said. "They know about him already."

By the time the boys got there, I had just barely persuaded her. Everyone came crowding into the small room, and Diana glanced up at them.

"He's very cool," said Evan as he watched the iguana crawl up to the top of Diana's knee.

"He's like my own little dragon," said Diana, more to Iggy than anyone else. She gave him some watercress, and we all watched him eat. Diana gradually warmed up with all the attention, though she wouldn't talk to Lauren, who looked at me and shrugged when she realized Diana was still mad.

After he ate, we sat around and let him perch on our shoulders and walk around on our arms and legs. Lauren took videos. Diana showed the boys how the iguana loved getting its chin scratched.

"We have to take the iguana out in the sun today," Diana said. "We read online that iguana hatchlings have to have vitamin D."

"Hatchlings?"

"That's what they call baby iguanas. But we have to somehow keep him hidden while we do that."

"I'm in!" Guy said. "We can sit near the pool and position our stuff around it so nobody can see it. This is going to be cool. The day of the iguana. The iguana caper. The Iwannaguana caper."

Evan laughed, repeating, "The Iwannaiguana caper!"

Evan and Guy stood up.

"We'll meet you guys out by the pool," Lauren said. "Find some chairs in the sun, and save us some."

"Okay! See you in a little while." Evan and Guy ducked through the door.

As soon as they left, I tried to talk to Diana and Lauren.

"I really think we need to tell Daddy and Lynn about it," I said. "Maybe people are looking for it."

"Do you think he's really valuable?" Lauren said, videotaping as Iggy climbed over Diana's knee.

I was also starting to get worried about Grammy's birthday celebration tonight. I wanted it to be good. We needed to take some time to write her a poem or a song, not just spend all our time playing with the iguana.

Diana and Lauren were touching the lizard and holding him, and he seemed to like to sit on their shoulders and crawl on them. I couldn't bring myself to touch him. I didn't know how his skin would feel, and I was afraid he might bite me.

"Let's just wait and see," Lauren said. "It's so cool to have him here to play with, isn't it?"

"You're such a worrywart, Stephanie," Diana said. "Chill."

Twenty minutes later, after we were all in our bathing suits ready to go to the pool, Diana slipped Iggy into her beach bag.

Having Iggy out by the pool was easier than we thought. We put five chairs together over in one sunny corner and piled all of our beach bags in the center of them. Then we sat on the lounge chairs and Diana opened her beach bag and let Iggy crawl out. The moment he crawled out into the sun, he blinked and settled in for some sunbathing.

"Wow, his skin looks darker when he's out in the sun," Diana said.

There were some potted hibiscus plants beside the pool, and Diana went over, picked a few of the crepey red flowers, and brought them back to where we were sitting.

"So this is what my mom did once when she was in Saint Thomas. She said iguanas love hibiscus flowers." She held out a flower to Iggy, and he eagerly ate some of it. He was having trouble eating the big petals on the flower, so Diana took it back and tore it into smaller pieces. "Check it out! He does like it!"

We spent awhile sitting in the sun with Iggy. He was skittish and liked to be able to run into Diana's beach bag. He sat at the edge of it in the sunshine, and whenever someone walked by and cast a shadow, he ran back inside.

We hadn't been at the pool long when Luke came out with a couple of friends and threw his towel on a lounge chair near us. One of his friends yelled, "Geronimo!" and jumped into the pool, and the others followed him, sending up walls of water and splashing us.

"Luke!" we yelled in annoyed voices.

"Be careful not to let Luke see Iggy," Lauren said to Diana. "He loves critters. He'll become obsessed, and he might tell Mom and Dad."

Diana nodded, catching Iggy and putting him back in the beach bag. Once Luke and his friends were occupied playing basketball in the pool, she let Iggy out again.

A little bit later, I saw Daddy and Lynn coming up the stairs to the pool.

"Diana! Daddy and Lynn are coming!"

Quickly, Diana scooped Iggy back into her beach bag and zipped it up. She gave me a threatening look. "Now don't tell them!" she hissed.

"Hey, kids!" Daddy said. "This ship is so big, we never see you! Are these new friends of yours?"

Evan and Guy quickly scrambled to their feet and introduced themselves, shaking hands with Daddy.

"Nice to meet you, sir," Guy said.

"So what kind of trouble have you kids been getting into today?" Daddy asked. "I bet you boys have been back to the buffet a few times!"

"Yessir," said Evan. "We're eating as much as we can."

"Tonight is our celebration for Grammy's birthday," Lynn reminded us. "Do you girls have your gifts ready? Remember, your gifts don't need to cost money. They just need to have TLC."

"Right." Lauren nodded. "We're going to write her a poem this afternoon."

My heart was beating furiously, and I tried not to look at the beach bag.

"So, I'm so glad you girls are hanging out together, and that you've made some friends," Lynn said, touching Diana on the shoulder. Diana pulled away.

There was an uncomfortable silence. I swallowed and stared at a spot on the ground. Would Daddy be able to somehow tell that Guy had kissed me? Lauren and Diana stared at the pool, and Guy and Evan shifted their weight from one foot to another, their hands in their bathing-suit pockets.

A moment later Lynn took Daddy's hand. "Let's leave the kids alone, Norm," she said. "I can see it's making them antsy for us to be here at the teen pool."

"Yeah, this is the TEEN pool," Lauren said jokingly. "Only TEENS allowed at the TEEN pool."

Lynn and Daddy headed back to the stairs. The minute they left, I watched Diana heave a sigh of relief. I was feeling guilty, though, knowing that we were keeping a secret from them. And I knew they wouldn't like it that I had kissed Guy.

There was a moment awhile later when Iggy was startled by a shadow and went skittering across the pool deck. Diana jumped to her feet and raced after him.

Iggy ran up to a step and tried to make the leap up the step but missed, and that was when Diana got him. She raced back to our chairs and put him into the beach bag, zipping it up.

At that moment, the American we had seen talking with Manuel walked by with a tray of Cokes for some people a short distance away, and he gave Diana and her beach bag a searching look, but he didn't stop to say anything.

"I'm going to take him back in," she said. "I don't know whether he's had enough sun, but I'm afraid he's going to get away."

Lauren and I were left with the boys, and eventually we started talking about our families.

Guy lived with his mom, who hadn't remarried, and Evan's parents still lived together.

"So, what's it like to have a stepfather and a stepmother?" Guy asked. "I keep wondering what it's going to be like if mom meets someone. She's been dating on one of those online dating sites. She hasn't met anyone she really thinks is cool so far, but you never know."

"It was a real adjustment at first," I said honestly. "I had wanted things to stay the way they were. Even if Mama and Daddy weren't still in love, I didn't care! Now I know it's not good for them to be together. And I've started to get close to Diana, and that was unexpected." I could have said either an unexpected bonus or an unexpected challenge, and I decided just to leave it open-ended.

At that moment the American waiter who had walked by with the sodas came back with his empty tray. He stopped beside the potted hibiscus and stared at us for a moment. He didn't say anything to us, but I could feel my face going hot, and I became uncomfortable beneath his gaze.

Why was he staring at us?

Later, when we were going back to our room, I saw him again walking down the hall. Was he following us? He just nodded and said "Good afternoon."

Before Grammy's birthday celebration, Lauren had to turn in her videotape at the teen club so that Josh could broadcast it with the other teen videos. Diana wanted to stay with Iggy, but I went with Lauren.

On the way I asked Lauren about when she videotaped Guy and me. "Did you keep that? That's not on what you're turning in, is it?"

"Oh, I erased it," Lauren said. "I was just joking around. I would never keep anything like that. But I'm glad I didn't leave you two together for very long!" She poked me with her elbow.

"Nothing was going to happen!"

"Well, I made sure it didn't."

"You didn't have to babysit me."

"You're too boy crazy for your own good, Steph. You need your cousin to keep you in line!"

"No, I don't!" I set my jaw and glared at her.

By then we were at the teen club, and Josh greeted us.

"Hello, girls!" he said. "I wanted to say that unfortunately I wasn't able to get permission for you to tape in the employee quarters. I thought they'd be pretty strict about that, and I was right. Sorry."

"Well, it was worth a try," Lauren said. She handed him her memory card. "Here's my video," she said. "I interviewed our steward, Manuel."

"Nice," Josh said. "That's an approach we don't see often."

"Well, we just thought that the lives of the staff would be interesting," Lauren said.

"Hers is really good," I told Josh. I was mad at Lauren, but I wasn't going to let Josh see that. "The interview with Manuel will make you cry."

"Wow, I can't wait to see it," Josh said. "Tonight at

ten, we'll be broadcasting on the ship's channel all the videos that the teens made. Be sure to watch!"

"Great. See you later!"

A few hours later, we were in our room, tripping over each other getting ready for the dress-up dinner and Grammy's birthday party. Both of Lauren's dresses were lying on her bed, and all my hair products and makeup were all over mine. Even though we'd had disagreements today, the mood had changed when we started talking about Grammy's birthday celebration. We wanted to write a good poem for her. None of us wanted to mess it up. Even Diana had gotten into it and let us French-braid her hair again.

I had on my yellow sundress, Lauren really did look older in her one-shouldered blue dress, and Diana was wearing the purple empire style Lynn and I had bought her.

"That purple color is really in," I told Diana. "You look great."

She gave me a look of shy pleasure. "Do you really think so?"

"I do," I said as I buckled my strappy sandals. "I want to take pictures to show everyone at school what we looked like!"

When we met the rest of the family at our table in the restaurant, everyone made noises of appreciation.

"Three beautiful girls!" Grammy said.

"You look beautiful yourself, Grammy," I said, and she did. She was wearing her sparkly silver top, which matched her hair, and she wore a pair of pearl earrings that had been a gift from Granddaddy many years ago.

"Doesn't she look fabulous?" Daddy said, putting his arm around Grammy. "I feel so lucky to be able to be here with my wonderful mother on this special day."

Then Luis and Bogdan approached our table and wished Grammy a "Happy Birthday."

When we all sat down, Daddy suggested that we all join hands for a prayer. "Dear God," he said, "thank you for giving us this special time with Grammy and with each other. Thank you for giving us a lifetime with Grammy to allow her to share with us her joyous outlook on life. May we be as loving and forgiving toward each other as Grammy has been with us. Amen."

"Amen," we all said. Then Daddy proposed a toast to Grammy, and the grown-ups lifted their wine glasses while we kids lifted our water glasses.

"To Grammy, who has always put family first and has given of herself to each one of us in ways that have meant so much," Daddy said.

"To my mother, the woman to whom I owe everything and with whom I have the most complicated relationship on the planet!" said Aunt Carol.

"Cheers!" we all said.

"We wrote Grammy a poem," I said, and Lauren and Diana and I stood up. I was in the middle, holding the sheet of paper with the poem. We each had a few assigned lines to read.

To our Grammy …
She babysat when we were tykes
She knows everything that we like
She tells us what to do and say
It is Grammy's way or the highway
She is always full of cheer
But she doesn't ever drink beer
She lets us look through her jewelry box
She serves us bagels with cream cheese and lox,
She adores her little dog named Jelly
Who loves for you to scratch his belly.
She is always there to listen
A tear in her eye will sometimes glisten
No one could ever have a better Grammy
We love her so much it gives us a whammy.

The whole family clapped and laughed.

"Very entertaining!" said Daddy. "Though I wouldn't hold my breath to win any poetry awards."

Then we gave Grammy the birthday card we'd made

her. Lauren was a pretty good artist, and she drew a picture of Grammy with all four kids on the front of the card, and then we each wrote a note to her.

I wrote:

Dear Grammy,
You hold this family together. You are my idol of what a grandmother should be, and I love you more than words can say.
Love, Stephanie

Diana had written:

Dear Grammy,
You have made me feel like your own grand-daughter, like part of this family. Thank you.
Diana

Then the grown-ups gave her a small, elongated box with white wrapping and a silver ribbon. We didn't know about this gift! There was a hush as we all held our breath and Grammy's strong fingers untied the silver ribbon and pulled the paper away. When she opened the box, there was a gorgeous necklace with a pink stone that the grown-ups had bought for her.

"Oh, it's beautiful!" Grammy said, holding the necklace up in the air so all of us could see.

Luis and Bogdan then brought out a rich dark-chocolate birthday cake. Flickering on top of the cake were seven lit candles, and one that was shorter, one for each decade of Grammy's life, and the short one for the half-decade. The whole waitstaff gathered, with their brocade vests and white aprons, to sing "Happy Birthday" to Grammy. Grammy was smiling, but her face was wet with tears.

"I'm making a wish!" she said, closing her eyes. And she sat there for a minute, her arms in the air, her eyes closed, with the light from the candles dancing over her face and her sparkly silver top. And then she took a deep breath and blew out the candles.

Everyone in the dining room, from the waitstaff to the group at the farthest table, clapped and cheered.

When the noise finally died down, she said, "Thank you all for such a lovely birthday celebration. Nothing means more to me than being here together with the family. I love each one of you so very much."

Each of us took turns giving Grammy a hug. I noticed that even Diana didn't hang back.

13

DIANA

After dinner, when we were standing outside the restaurant, a TV in the hallway suddenly showed Josh from the teen club.

"Several of our teens shot and edited their own videos this week," he said, "and we'd like to show you a little of the work they did. The first video was shot and edited by Lauren Whitt, who is fourteen, and from Gaithersburg, Maryland."

I glanced over at Lauren, who had a huge grin on her face.

Then Lauren's video of Manuel faded in.

"Wow! Look, Lauren, they're showing your video!" Luke said.

The entire interview was shown, including Manuel's description of his job, his relationship with his wife and children, and his desire to save for hearing aids for Carlo. When the moment came and Manuel looked away from the camera to hide his emotion, I felt my face begin to get hot.

I had been so annoyed about Lauren shooting videos all the time but I could see now: Lauren's video was good. I hated to admit it. It made me see Manuel through different eyes. It almost made me cry.

"That's a good thing you did," Grammy said to Lauren, "making that video. Your video creates such empathy for Manuel's situation. It makes people feel for him."

"Thanks, Grammy." Lauren leaned close and put her arm around Grammy's waist. "I know some people think I'm obsessed with videotaping, but I think it's a fantastic way to communicate."

Was that me she was talking about, me thinking she was obsessed? I could feel myself getting mad. Did she mean me? The truth was, I had been holding myself back the whole cruise. There were so many times when I wanted to say something to her and I had bitten my tongue. Dr. Shrink would have been proud.

"At the end of the day," said Uncle Ted, "we're very proud of you, Lauren."

He said "at the end of the day." Was he saying that on purpose? To tell Lauren that it was okay that she and Stephanie made fun of him? So maybe he was saying that me mentioning it was wrong?

"We certainly are proud," said Aunt Carol, and the family applauded as Aunt Carol and Uncle Ted gave Lauren a hug.

"Yeah, we're proud, too," Stephanie said, glancing over at me

Now I had to say something! I looked at my feet, then looked over at Lauren.

"Yeah," was all I could say.

When it came time to leave, Stephanie offered to help Grammy carry her presents and cards and the rest of the cake to her room. I tensed up. That meant Lauren and I would be walking back to our room without her. We hadn't been together, just the two of us, the whole cruise.

I told the 'rents that I was going back to the room to finish my horse book. Lauren told hers that she might go to the teen club after changing out of her fancy dress. Good! Then I could be alone in the room with Iggy. As Lauren and I headed down the elevator together, I felt self-conscious being trapped in there with her and couldn't think of anything to say.

"Everybody loved my video," she said.

"Yeah. It was good," I said. So pat yourself on the back, why don't you? Talk about fishing for a compliment!

"Don't be jealous, now," she said in a light, teasing voice.

The elevator doors opened on our floor and she stepped out.

"Jealous? Why would I be jealous of you?" I said, stumbling out after her.

"Why? Oh, I don't know, I was just kidding," she said. "Maybe you're jealous that Stephanie and I have known each other our whole lives."

We were facing each other in the lobby beside the elevator, me in my purple dress with the frills, Lauren in her off the shoulder style. People were walking by, but I was so mad I didn't care.

"Maybe you're jealous of me!" I said. "Maybe you're jealous because now Stephanie and I are sisters and we will get closer than you could ever be!"

Lauren waved me off and started walking down the corridor. "You've only known each other for two years."

"So? That's being together, for the past few months, every day! You guys hardly ever see each other."

"Stephanie and I have been cousins since we were babies! I've been through her parents' divorce with her. We'll be close forever!"

"Stephanie and I will be stepsisters forever!" I said. The moment I said it I stopped. I hadn't until this very instant realized how strongly I felt.

Lauren didn't see me stop, and she kept walking down the corridor. After a minute she stopped and turned to face me, speaking loudly to cover the distance between us. "Stephanie is crazy about me. I bet she told you great things about me. Tell me what she said."

I answered quietly. "She said you were awesome and that I would love you."

There was a silence between us.

"What did she tell you about me?" I took a few steps closer.

"The same thing," Lauren said.

The silence drew out longer. Lauren and I stood, both of us out of breath, staring at each other. Moronic Mood-o-meter at about eight. Dr. Shrink would say to count to ten and take some deep breaths.

While I was counting, I started to feel embarrassed for acting the way I did, and looked away. About that time Lauren sighed and looked at her feet.

"Maybe we could just try a little harder," Lauren said at last.

"Okay," I agreed. My eyes were stinging. "I better go check on Iggy."

14

STEPHANIE

Once we put her necklace and cards away, Grammy gestured toward her balcony and said, "Honey, why don't you sit out on the balcony with me for a little while?"

"Okay," I said, walking outside. I hadn't really gotten much of a chance to talk to Grammy so far, and her advice meant a lot to me. I really wanted to talk to her about the disagreements between Lauren and Diana. I also wanted to talk to her about living with Daddy and Lynn.

There was a light breeze, and the lights from the ship bounced off the dark, choppy waves below. I could hear the low murmur of the voices of other people sitting on their balconies talking.

Grammy carefully grasped the arm of a chair, then lowered herself into it. "Now that I'm seventy-five, I'll have to be more careful about getting around," she said. "What you wrote on my card was really very sweet, Stephanie. I appreciate it."

"Did you like our silly poem?" I asked.

"Oh yes, it was very literary." Grammy laughed.

"I guess you can't tell what you wished for when you blew out your candles," I said teasingly.

"Oh, I don't mind telling," Grammy said. "I wished for God to watch over every one of you." She crossed her legs and leaned her cheek on her hand. "So, tell me how things are going now that you're living with your father. How did your mother take it?"

"She started crying," I said. I thought about Mama turning her face away from me and trying to wipe away the tears without me seeing. "And she misses me. It made me feel even more awful. But, you know, Barry's son, Matt, who flunked out of college last year, is living with them. I didn't like living with him, and I didn't like his friends." I didn't want to tell Grammy the details, about the beer they stole and drank or the

Adderall pills they were selling. Sometimes it's best not to tell older people everything.

"But your mother understood?"

"She told me she did, and she said that things were tough with Matt right now, and she wanted me to be happy. But on the weekends when I go back there to stay now, she makes special plans for us, and she always seems so sad when it's time for me to leave. Last time I visited, she said maybe once Matt is on his own again I can move back."

"Do you think you will?"

I took a deep breath. "I don't know. I'm tired of moving around. I wish I could just stay in one place," I said honestly. "I feel like I've settled in at Daddy's, and I'd like to stay there."

"Well, then that's what you need to say to people," Grammy said. "What you did wasn't easy, Stephanie, and I'm proud of you for standing up for yourself."

"Thanks, that means a lot, Grammy." Waves splashed faintly against the sides of the ship. A soft breeze threaded through our hair.

"What about you and Diana?" The breeze picked up a little, and Grammy pulled her wrap a bit more tightly around her.

"We're getting along better and better," I said. "This

trip has been a challenge, though, because she and Lauren keep having fights."

"I'm sorry to hear that!" Grammy said. "What kind of fights?"

Then I was sorry I said that. Maybe Grammy would ask for more details, and I would have to lie about the iguana. But I told her about the fight over Uncle Ted's "the end of the day" sayings, and surprisingly, it seemed as though she already knew what had happened.

"I can see you've tried very hard to have a good relationship with Diana, and I'm proud of you for doing that," Grammy said. "It's important in life to work at our relationships. They're everything we've got. That's what I always say, Stephanie. God has given us others to love. Life is relationships and what we make of them."

I examined my hands in my lap. I had suddenly remembered the kids at school calling Diana "annn-i-mal," and the fact that it was because of something I had said. I couldn't seem to forget that. And I remembered what Guy had said about taking responsibility for what I had done.

"Grammy, I did something I'm not proud of," I said. Her face was hard to see in the dark.

"What's that, honey?"

"I was mad at Diana one day because she was rude, and I told a friend of mine that Diana liked animals more than people. She must have told someone else about it, because a few days later, some of the people at school were calling her 'annn-i-mal' in really mean voices. Her feelings were so hurt about it, and I think it was because of me saying that about her."

Grammy was silent for a minute. "Things like that can happen. That's really unfortunate. You didn't do it on purpose, but what you said caused damage."

She didn't tell me it was okay that I had done it. That's one thing I liked about talking to Grammy. She was honest. She didn't just try to make you feel okay about things.

"Have you apologized to her?"

I shook my head. "I haven't even admitted that I think it was me that started it. She doesn't know." I hadn't even said anything to Daddy about it. I had kept it a deep dark secret. Except for Guy.

"Well—" said Grammy.

Suddenly there was a knock on Grammy's door. Grammy grasped the arms of her chair to get up, but I said, "That's okay, I'll get it," and I jumped up and ran to the door. When I opened it, Diana was there. Her face was twisted with deep distress.

"Iggy's gone!" she hissed.

"Oh no!"

"What's wrong?" came Grammy's voice.

I glanced back and saw Grammy stand up and come to the balcony entrance.

Diana came in, whispering. "I've looked everywhere in the room. He's not in there. He's either escaped or someone has taken him."

15

DIANA

I looked at Stephanie's shocked face and saw Grammy's expression of confusion, and I decided I never should have come to Grammy's room to tell Stephanie about Iggy. Now we had no choice but to tell Grammy everything.

"What's wrong?" Grammy said again.

I thought about little Iggy, wedged in a corner hiding somewhere. Or maybe whoever had smuggled him onto the ship had come into our room and found him and stolen him back. How had they found him? How would the smugglers treat him? They thought of him just as a way to make money, not as a wild creature that should be free. Maybe they would mistreat him in some way.

Stephanie looked at me, wide-eyed, with a question on her face.

"I have to go, Grammy," Stephanie said. "We have an emergency."

"What kind of emergency?" Grammy said, crossing the room, directing her question at me.

I hesitated. I *had* promised Stephanie that I would tell about Iggy after Grammy's birthday celebration.

I sat down on Grammy's bed. "We found something," I said. "And now we've lost it," I added.

"Why don't you tell me the whole story," Grammy said.

So I told her everything, about finding Iggy and about hiding him for the past two days. I told her what we'd found out about blue iguanas from the Blue Iguana Recovery Programme website. I told her about taking Iggy out on the sundeck today so he could get vitamin D from sunshine.

"So, anyway," I concluded, "someone must have smuggled him onto the ship from Grand Cayman. And they must have been looking for him while we had him. And now they've either taken him back or he's escaped. Will you promise not to tell Mom and Norm?"

"No, I won't promise!" Grammy said sternly. "This is nothing to kid around about! I'm glad you don't have the iguana anymore. What you've been doing could be a criminal act. You could end up in jail."

Stephanie and I sat next to each other on Grammy's bed. Stephanie chewed her fingernail, which was something she did when she was nervous or upset.

"You just leave well enough alone. Don't you get mixed up with those smugglers."

"But Grammy," Stephanie said, "one of them is Manuel, the steward that Lauren interviewed on the videotape. You saw what a loving father he is. He would do anything for his son."

"Maybe that's the key," Grammy said. "That he would do anything for him. Even something that isn't legal."

Stephanie hung her head. "I guess. I just can't think of him as a bad guy."

She stood up. "Please don't tell Daddy and Lynn, Grammy! We didn't know what we were doing was wrong," she pleaded.

My heart pounded when I realized that Stephanie had said "we."

Grammy gave us a deep and thoughtful look. "I will

leave it up to you to tell your parents about this your-selves," she said slowly. "But if you don't, I'll have to."

Stephanie and I nodded. I stretched and pretended to yawn. "Well, it's getting late. We better get back to our room, Steph," I said.

"All right. I'm trusting you girls now," Grammy said. "Give me a hug good night," she said. Stephanie let Grammy fold her into her arms and stayed there while Grammy patted her back a couple of times. I felt shyer about a hug from Grammy and stood back.

"Come on, you too!" Grammy said in a bossy voice. So I stepped forward, and she wrapped me in her arms and squeezed. I felt the warmth of Grammy's arms around me, and then her lips brushed my cheek. "There. Now you girls go and do the right thing," she said.

As soon as we left Grammy's room, Stephanie grabbed my arm. "What should we do?" she said.

"Let's look for Iggy in our room once more," I said as we ran down the narrow corridor. "If he's not there, we'll have to try to figure out who took him."

We raced to the stair landing and down the stairs to our room level. As soon as we got back to the room, Lauren greeted us. Ever since our fight, Lauren and I had been getting along so much better.

"There's no sign of him anywhere," she said. "I've looked in every corner."

Just to be safe, I looked all through my bunk and everywhere in the bathroom again. "I left him closed in the shower," I said. "I don't see how he could've gotten out. I think someone came and got him."

"Remember the American steward we saw talking to Manuel in the employee cafeteria?" Stephanie asked. "I saw him out by the pool today after you left, Diana. He was staring at us. And then I saw him again when we were on our way back to the room. Maybe he saw Iggy and was following us to find out where we were keeping him."

The three of us froze and were silent. I was thinking about what it might feel like to be followed.

"So after Manuel comes by our room tonight," Lauren said, "one of us has to follow him."

"I will," I said. I thought about Dad then, wishing I could tell him about this cruise and the adventure we were having with the iguana. Dad would want me to be fearless and bold.

"I have a question," Stephanie said. "If someone does something wrong or illegal in order to do something good, does that still count as doing something wrong? Do you think God would forgive Manuel for smuggling the iguana if he was doing it to get the money to help his son?"

"You mean sort of like Robin Hood, rob from the rich to give to the poor?" Lauren asked.

"Yeah," Stephanie said. "Is it still wrong?"

"I think it is," Lauren said. "It doesn't change the fact that what he's doing is against the law. What do you think, Diana?"

"I think people should have to pay for what they do," I said honestly. But it was a hard question. And Stephanie didn't agree with me.

"I feel like what Manuel is doing," Stephanie said, "he's doing out of love. When a person does something out of love, even if it's wrong, that has to be taken into consideration," Stephanie said.

"So you don't think he should have to pay?" I said.

"I just think that things aren't always black and white," she said.

I think that Stephanie thought forgiveness was the key to relationships. Last spring, when we had been at the Outer Banks, Stephanie had talked to me about how she felt about forgiveness. She thought that I should have forgiven our friend Cody for the mistake he made. Eventually I did say good-bye to him, even though I had a hard time forgiving him.

I didn't know whether Stephanie going back to church had to do with what she thought about forgiveness. I just knew that I was confused. If Manuel had smuggled the iguana onto the ship, then he had broken the law. How could we change that? And shouldn't he pay for what he had done? What difference did it even make if we forgave him?

There was a soft knock on our door.

"Come in," Stephanie said.

The door opened, and Manuel stood in the doorway with his uniform on. "I am here to do the turndown this evening. And would you girls like some mints before bed?" he asked, holding a small white tray with foil-wrapped mints. The expression on his face was unreadable. But he seemed more stiff, a little bit more defensive than he had been in the past few days.

"Sure," Stephanie said with her most welcoming smile, glancing over at me.

I tried to imagine what he must think of us, if he had indeed come and gotten the iguana from us. I wondered where he might be keeping it, if it had room to walk around.

"Do you have our iguana?" I blurted out.

Stephanie put her hand over her mouth.

"Pardon me?" Manuel said politely, raising his eyebrows.

"We found an iguana, and we were keeping it here in our room. We think it's a rare iguana and that someone was smuggling it from Grand Cayman to the United States. But it's disappeared. Have you seen it?"

I watched Manuel's face carefully. His expression

changed briefly, and then his polite, distant expression returned.

"I am sorry, I do not know what you are talking about," Manuel said. "Animals are not allowed on board ship."

Was he lying to us, or was he telling us the truth?

"Well, we don't have one now because someone took it. Someone came into our room this afternoon. It's gone," I said.

"We found out by doing research that if you smuggle an endangered species into the U.S., you can go to jail for up to five years," Lauren said.

Manuel's face changed for an instant, then his distant, polite expression came back, as he sighed deeply. "I am sorry. As I said before, I do not know what you are talking about."

On past nights Manuel had asked us questions about our day on the cruise as he worked, but tonight he simply gave us our mints and emptied the trash wordlessly.

"Did you have a good day, Manuel?" Stephanie asked, a little shyly.

"It was fine," Manuel said matter-of-factly, without a smile. "I work all day, as usual."

"Did you get a chance to talk to your children today?" Stephanie persisted.

"No, I did not," Manuel said. "Two of the children were feeling sick today, and my wife could not Skype."

He neatly folded back the coverlets on our beds and then turned to the door.

"Aren't you going to fold any towel animals tonight, Manuel?" Stephanie asked. "We love it when you do that."

Manuel's shoulders slumped, and he hesitated with his hand on the doorknob. Then he turned back to us. "Of course." I thought of all that wasn't being said tonight in our room as Manuel did his duties. *Are you telling us the truth? Did you take the iguana from us? Where are you keeping it now? How much money is it worth? Are you doing it for your son?*

He went into the hallway and brought back fresh towels, and while we watched, he folded two towels into an animal that could have been an alligator. But it also could have been an iguana.

He left the alligator/iguana on the desk.

"Have a nice evening, ladies," he said.

After he shut the door, there was silence in our room for a long moment.

"Did you think he acted guilty?He was more serious than usual," Stephanie said.

I jumped to my feet. "I'm going to follow him to his room and see if he's telling us the truth."

"I'll go with you!" said Lauren, jumping up with the video camera.

"You can't bring the video camera," I said quickly.

"Okay, I won't bring the camera. I just want to come," Lauren said. She sat down heavily on the bed while Stephanie began twisting her hair nervously.

"I don't think you should go, Diana. I think we should just forget about everything," Stephanie said. "Pretend nothing happened."

"But someone has Iggy! I don't believe he could have gotten out of the shower today! And someone's going to smuggle him! We have to save him!" I said.

I eased the door open and looked out into the hall. "Manuel's cart is a few doors down," I whispered. "I'm going to go hide in the supply room."

Lauren and I stood by the door, ready to sneak out.

"Wait, don't leave me here by myself," Stephanie said. "I'll come!"

"Okay, hurry up!" Lauren said.

We tiptoed around Manuel's cart down to the supply room and hid behind a big hamper of used towels. A moment later he came out of the room and headed toward us down the corridor with his cart. As he stored his cart in the supply room, we remained completely still, hiding behind another cart. A minute or so after he left the supply room, the three of us sneaked into the corridor, and then raced soundlessly down the hall, stopping at the entryway where he'd turned. The entryway led to the cargo elevator.

We waited until the doors closed, then looked up to see which floor he was going to by what number was lit up above the door. Five! We ran to the stairs, then went racing down, two steps at a time, to the fifth floor. We burst out of the stairwell and back out into the corridor to see Manuel just disappearing through the set of doors that said Employees Only.

We waited a few seconds after the doors swung shut behind him, then raced through.

We kept our distance, running on tiptoe down the corridor until he turned a corner. I stopped and held a finger to my lips, then peeked around the corner. He was putting his key card into his door.

We waited until he had gone inside, then tiptoed toward the room.

"Listen," I said. "See if we can hear anything."

I put my ear to the door and heard muffled but rising voices inside.

"What did you do?" Manuel said. "Why did you not tell me?"

"I didn't have time," Ryan said.

"Did you know we could go to jail for five years?"

"That's if you get caught. Hardly anybody gets

caught!" Ryan said. "I'll just tape it inside my sock, and then I'm off to Miami and several thousand dollars."

"What will you feed it?"

"Who cares? Don't worry about it. We dock in the morning."

They weren't going to feed Iggy! I could feel anger flashing behind my eyes.

"I care!" Manuel said. "I have changed my mind. These kids know about the iguana. They could tell the captain. I do not want to go to jail."

"Give me that!"

We stood wide-eyed as we heard a struggle inside the room. Suddenly, with a tumbling of locks and a jerk, the door was wrenched open. The three of us jumped back as Manuel lunged through the door holding a jar. Inside the jar was Iggy, looking gray and limp.

"What are you doing here?" he yelled.

"Oh my gosh, he'll suffocate!" I shouted.

At that second, Ryan reached through the door for the jar, but Manuel jerked it away, running several steps down the hallway. The top flew off the jar, and Iggy slid onto the floor.

My heart leaped to my throat. Poor Iggy! I elbowed my way past Manuel, but Iggy had taken off down the hall, scampering and skittering from one side of the corridor to another.

"Go, Iggy!" I yelled.

Manuel and I both ran down the hall after him. I could hear Ryan's heavy footfalls behind me. Two employees were coming the other way, and their faces took on looks of amazement. They plastered themselves against the wall as Iggy scampered by, and then we raced by after him.

"Somebody catch him!" Stephanie squealed.

16

STEPHANIE

Icouldn't believe Iggy had gotten away! Now all of us were running down the corridor after him. The corridor opened up to a landing with stairs and an elevator, and Iggy veered onto the landing, and then began scrambling up the stairs.

I was terrified someone was going to step on him!

We raced upstairs right behind him, but it was amazing how he could leap once he got started. I glanced behind me and saw that Lauren had brought the video camera after all. She was taping everything that happened!

Iggy skittered up to the next landing, then darted into the employee bar, which was full of people having drinks after a long day of work.

"Catch him!" Manuel said to people sitting at a table as Iggy ran under the table legs.

A woman screamed and jumped to her feet. "What is that?"

Diana was close behind, and she zigzagged past another table to block Iggy from heading that way. Iggy veered away from her and raced underneath another table.

"Get it!" Ryan yelled.

Everyone at the table leaped to their feet, knocking chairs over, and Manuel got down on his stomach and tried reaching under the table, but Iggy was too fast for him and skittered to the corner of the room.

"What is it?" people were asking.

Then he was cornered. Manuel and Diana both dropped to their hands and knees and crawled toward him.

"Come on, Diana, get him!" I said, coming up close behind her. Ryan had found a broom and was trying to sweep him out.

"Be careful!" Diana yelled. "You'll hurt him!"

He swiped at Iggy, who leaped in the air and landed right on my thigh!

I screamed.

"Stephanie, get him before he gets away!" Diana shouted.

I looked at his golden eyes and tense trembling body. Could I make myself touch him? I held my breath. Then I grabbed him. When I felt his dry, cool skin, I almost let go, but I made myself hold on. Putting my fingers underneath his front legs, I picked him up. His eyes darted about frantically, and I could feel his little heart pounding inside his body. Gasping, I handed him to Diana.

"Nice work, Steph!" Diana said. She pulled him close and cradled him against her chest.

Suddenly I heard a voice behind me.

"What seems to be going on here?"

I turned around and saw the head of ship security in his uniform right behind me.

"These girls smuggled an iguana on board the ship from Grand Cayman!" said Ryan loudly. "It got away, and we were trying to catch it!"

I covered my mouth with my hand.

"No, we didn't!" Diana cried.

"They did!" said Lauren, pointing at Ryan.

The security officer crossed his arms over his chest. "Let's take this to my office right now," he said.

A few minutes later, all five of us, including Diana holding Iggy, were seated in the security director's office. The name on the outside of his office and his name tag said Officer Decker.

"All right," said Officer Decker, "I want to hear from the employees first. What is this animal and how did it get on board?"

After a few tense seconds, Manuel sighed deeply and sat down in the chair by the desk. "A few weeks ago, Ryan told me that he knew an American who would pay a lot of money for a blue iguana. They are so rare, they are practically extinct. He told me if I could help him get one, he would give me half the money. My son needs hearing aids, and I am desperate for money, so I said okay. I did research on the places in Grand Cayman where the wild iguanas live. This past visit, when we docked on Grand Cayman, we sneaked up on the iguana and grabbed it from a low branch on a tree."

"And then you smuggled the iguana onto the ship?" asked Officer Decker.

Manuel nodded. "I taped it inside my sock. But it took us longer than we thought to catch it. Those little creatures are fast as they race up tree trunks and across the forest floor. I ended up being late getting back to the ship, so I was not able to return to my room before I came back to the passenger deck to do my evening duties. I had the iguana taped to my leg inside my sock, but I did not tape it securely enough. It got loose and crawled out of my sock and escaped not far from these girls' cabin. I have not seen it since, until just now." Manuel ran his hand over his face. "I assume the girls found it and kept it in their room."

"Yes," Diana said. "For almost two days. I was feeding it from the buffet."

"We took the iguana up on deck this afternoon to get some sun because we read they need vitamin D to survive. And I saw him up there watching us," I said to Officer Decker, pointing to Ryan.

Ryan pressed his lips together but didn't say anything.

"When we got back to our room tonight, Iggy was gone," Diana said. "I think one of them came into our room and stole him. We followed Manuel back to his room after he finished his steward duties and heard them arguing about the iguana. Then Manuel came out of the room with the iguana in a jar, and it got away."

"I have all that on video," Lauren offered. "You can see Manuel coming out of their room with the iguana in the jar."

"Did you take the iguana from the girls' room?" Officer Decker asked Ryan.

Ryan pressed his lips together and refused to answer.

"Yes, he did," said Manuel. "I changed my mind. I only did it to help raise money for my son's hearing aids. I did not realize I could do jail time. The lizard is so small!"

"It can grow to over five feet long," Diana said. "The iguana needs to go back to Grand Cayman and live in the wild. It's illegal to keep blue iguanas as pets."

"So, let me see this iguana," said Officer Decker, peering across his desk at Diana holding Iggy.

"Do you want to hold him? Be careful. He can get away."

"Not just yet," said Officer Decker. "And you say this iguana is extremely rare, practically extinct?"

"The only place blue iguanas live is on Grand Cayman," Diana said. "There are only about six hundred and fifty of them in the entire world. He needs to go back to Grand Cayman where he belongs."

Officer Decker rubbed his face thoughtfully. "Well, we're going back to Grand Cayman tomorrow after we dock. We could return it then."

"Oh, could you? That would be the best news ever."

"I imagine we need to do more than simply release the iguana when we arrive."

"There is a special group of people on Grand Cayman that take care of the iguanas, and I could call or email them, and maybe someone could meet the ship and take Iggy back to his habitat." Diana, with excitement, raked her hair behind her ear. "I can tell you how to feed him. He likes just about any vegetable, from kale to carrots."

"All right, then," said Officer Decker. "I am sure someone can handle this."

"Oh, it's very important that whoever takes him gives him a chance to get some sun. Iguanas need their sunbaths! Hey, maybe I should keep him until I get off the ship tomorrow?"

"That's okay. Can you get me the phone number or the email address of the blue-iguana people in Grand Cayman? We might even have an aquarium or terrarium around here where we can keep him temporarily for the couple of days it will take us to get back to Grand Cayman." Officer Decker stood up. "Okay, girls, you may go. We can take it from here. Gentlemen, you stay here."

"Oh, and he likes to have his chin scratched," Diana added.

"He does, does he?" said Officer Decker. "Well, it's time to say your farewells."

Diana held Iggy's face up close to hers. He cocked his head, looking like he was smiling again. "Bye, Iggy." She cradled him against her chest. "You be good now."

Iggy blinked his golden eyes and moved his front legs, trying to get away.

"You've got to watch him every minute," Diana said. "I kept him in the shower with the door closed. It's best if you hold him just behind his head."

"We'll keep that in mind," said Officer Decker. "Thanks."

And so we left Iggy in Officer Decker's office. I couldn't meet Manuel's eye as we walked out.

"What time is it?" Daddy was in his pj's, and Diana, Lauren, and I were sitting at the foot of his and Lynn's bed in their cabin. He squinted at the clock on his nightstand and rubbed his hand over his eyes. "You found what?"

"A blue iguana. A crew member smuggled it onto the ship from Grand Cayman, and then it got away. I found it in the hallway outside our room," Diana said.

"And you kept it in your cabin for two days?" Lynn said. "Without telling anyone?"

"Yes, but we just turned it over to ship security, and they're returning it to Grand Cayman," I said quickly. "We found out that it's a felony to bring one into the United States," I added. "You can go to jail for five years."

"Five years! A felony!" Daddy sat up and put his head in his hands.

"And we didn't want to do that," I concluded.

Lynn put on her robe and tied the belt around her waist. "I remember reading to you girls about the blue iguanas being among the endangered species that live on Grand Cayman. But I never dreamed that you'd actually be taking care of one."

"We actually prevented a crime from being committed," I said.

Daddy closed his eyes. "That is the best news I've heard so far tonight."

It was the wee morning hours, but back in our room none of us could sleep. We relived chasing Iggy down the ship's corridor and through the employee bar. We discussed every minute of our interview in Officer Decker's office.

"What do you think will happen to Ryan and Manuel?" I asked, pulling my sheet up over my chest.

"They'll probably be fired," Lauren said. "And maybe they'll have to go to jail."

"I feel so terrible," I said. "I liked Manuel."

"They smuggled the iguana," said Diana. "They have to take the consequences of their actions."

"Still," I said. "I still feel terrible."

The next morning before we got off the ship, Diana and I took the phone number of the Blue Iguana Recovery

Programme to Officer Decker, who dialed the number right away. He'd put Iggy in a giant clear plastic container from the kitchen. Two little cups the kitchen used for ketchup were in the container, holding water and an assortment of vegetables.

"Hello?" Officer Decker introduced himself and explained the situation. "It seems we have a rare baby iguana. What's that you call it ... a hatchling? A rare iguana hatchling here on our ship. One of our employees smuggled it onto our ship from your island. We are on our way back to Grand Cayman, and we are prepared to return the hatchling when we dock in two days' time. Will that be satisfactory? So a representative will meet our ship. Splendid. Do we know how to care for it? A young lady here has apparently done some research on the topic, and she has instructed me to give it vegetables from the buffet and to take it outside for a sunbath each day. Is there anything else I need to know?... Splendid. Thank you." He hung up. "All set. Iggy will be taken care of."

Diana seemed happy as we headed back to the room. She chattered about Iggy's future in the wild. Now that we were together without Lauren, I thought maybe this was my chance to tell her how sorry I was that I had started the rumor that caused people to call her "annn-i-mal." Both Guy and Grammy had advised me to admit it to her and apologize. That was the right thing to do. But she was so happy! And when I told her, I was sure she'd get so mad. Now that things were good, I didn't want to stir up trouble. I could always talk to her about it later.

So I didn't say anything. Was that bad? I wondered what God might think about that, and I hoped he would forgive me.

When Diana and I got back to the room, we found Lauren inside packing up her stuff. Manuel, knocked on our door.

"Thank you for all you have done for me," he said to us. "Words cannot express my gratitude."

"What do you mean?" I asked. I felt so guilty for what might have happened to him.

"The videotape that was shown last night," he began. And as we were standing there, a man came up to Manuel in the corridor.

"Last night I saw the videotape about you and your son," the man said. "I was moved and touched. I know what it's like to want something for your child and not be able to get it for them." He handed Manuel an envelope. "Here. This is to help with your son's hearing aids."

Manuel had a look of amazement on his face. He opened the envelope. Inside was a hundred-dollar bill.

At that moment a woman came up. She handed Manuel a second envelope. "I saw the video too. Here."

There was more money in the second envelope. Tears came to Manuel's eyes.

"Oh, thank you," he said, beginning to sob. "Thank you so very much."

Seeing Manuel's joy and gratitude, I could feel tears stinging my own eyes. Diana and I looked at Lauren and smiled.

"I do not know how to thank you for what you have done," Manuel said to us. "I will probably lose my job, and perhaps I will have to go to jail, but at least my son will have his hearing aids."

That was when I felt like we had done the right thing.

Later, we ran into Guy and Evan in the buffet line for breakfast, and we all sat together. Guy quickly used his diabetes kit, in his lap, to test himself and bolus.

"You are never going to believe all that's happened," Lauren told them. "We caught the guys that smuggled the iguana onto the ship!"

"No way!" said Evan.

It was pandemonium while we were telling them.

"We followed Manuel back to his room—" said Lauren.

"That's where they were keeping the iguana—" Diana continued.

"And Manuel came out with the iguana in a jar—" I added.

"And Iggy got away," Diana said.

Lauren continued, "—and then we chased Iggy all around the ship—"

"—and I finally caught him!" I said.

"Can you believe Stephanie caught him?" Diana said. "I was proud of her. She had refused to touch him the whole time."

"Good job!" Guy said. "Gimme five!" We slapped hands, laughing.

"And so, anyway, the security officer on the ship is going to take Iggy back to Grand Cayman and give him to the people from the Blue Iguana Recovery Programme. They're meeting the boat," Diana said. "I wish I could have kept Iggy, but I realize he's a wild animal and should be in the wild. Most of the time we had Iggy, he was gray-looking. When they're happy and confident, they turn blue, and we didn't see him blue much. I hope when he gets home, he'll be blue again. I'll miss Iggy, but I told Officer Decker how to feed Iggy and everything. Anyway," she said, standing up, "I better go finish packing. We have to have our luggage ready to go soon." She looked at Guy and Evan. "It was nice meeting you guys," she said.

"Same here," said Guy.

Eventually, everyone had left except Guy and me. I felt aware of him sitting next to me, with his elbow on the table close to mine. I had memorized his Grand Cayman T-shirt with the turtle on it, and the pair of wrinkled khakis and the rainbow flip-flops he wore.

Then a silence fell between us. I remembered the kiss, how soft his lips had felt, and I felt goosebumps on the back of my neck.

The thought came into my head that I probably would never see him again.

He started twirling an empty glass on his tray, and I wondered if he was thinking the same thing.

I could feel my heart beating in my throat.

He tossed his hair off his forehead. "So ... heading home," he said. "Are you on Facebook?"

"No," I said. "It was okay with Mama, but Daddy thinks I'm too young. I can't do it until I'm sixteen."

"Oh. Well, we could call or text."

"Okay." I had just gotten my cell phone out after not using it for the whole trip. We exchanged cell-phone numbers.

"I'm glad we had a chance to hang out."

"Me too." I twirled my phone on the table nervously. "Well, next time you sing karaoke, think of me," I said, smiling.

"I will!" He smiled. "And when you think of *Pirates of the Caribbean*, think of me!"

I hesitated. "That was my first kiss."

He looked at me. "Really?"

"Yeah. So I'll always remember you."

"Wow," he said.

"It'll be a good memory. You're really a kind person. And I'll remember your advice about Diana too."

"I'll remember you too, Stephanie."

We stood up, and as we walked across the dining hall together, my mind was racing. *This is the last time I'm ever going to see him,* I thought.

We stood in front of the elevators as people hurried by carrying packages of photos and other last-minute shipboard purchases before disembarking.

I was shaking a little bit as I looked into Guy's eyes, and I could tell he was trying to think of a way to maybe kiss me again. Part of me wanted him to, but another part of me didn't want to do it in a public place like this with all these people rushing by.

Then he seemed to make a decision. He kissed the tip of his finger and touched it to my forehead.

"See you later," he said.

"You too."

And so neither of us said good-bye.

17

DIANA

A half hour later, Stephanie, Lauren, and I had packed up our suitcases and put them out in the hallway for the stewards to take, as we were instructed.

"Hey, let's go up on deck and look around one last time before we leave," Lauren said.

We went up the elevator to the top floor. Lauren didn't have the video camera with her this time, and I thought about how mad I had gotten at her for wanting to videotape all the time. I wasn't mad anymore.

Lauren and I would never be close like her and Stephanie, but we had figured out how to respect each other and work together to keep the peace. Stephanie had helped to show us that.

We walked out onto the upper deck and saw Port Everglades spread out before us. We'd sailed all night and had docked early this morning. The waves rolled in at the foot of the high-rises, and the sun sparkled in their rows upon rows of windows.

"It's so strange to go to bed with water all around you and then wake up in the morning and be docked," I said.

"I know," said Stephanie. "That is so weird."

"This has been an amazing trip," Lauren said.

"It sure has," Stephanie said. "I can't believe I touched an iguana!" She was quieter than her usual self, though. I wondered what she might be thinking about.

"I can't believe you did either!" I told her. "You were like a hero!"

I could see Lauren glance at me, and I wondered if she thought that I might say she'd been a hero too, since she had taken the videotapes. And I had to admit, taking those videotapes had ended up being a good thing for her to do. I took a deep breath.

The warm Florida breeze whipped our hair around

our faces. One of the other cruise ships blew its horn, long and loud and deep.

Finally I said to Lauren, "You were like a hero too, Lauren, with the videotape. Without it we might never have been able to convince Officer Decker that Ryan and Manuel were the ones who smuggled Iggy. Also, we never would have been able to help Manuel get the money for his son. I'm sorry I kept saying that the videotaping was getting on my nerves. It ended up really making a difference."

I wondered what Dr. Shrink would say about what I just said. It hadn't been easy to say it. I cut my eyes at Lauren and kind of held my breath.

"Well, thanks," Lauren said. "I know I'm obsessed, and I need to work on that, but it's really great that it helped." She hesitated, then went on. "And you were a kind of hero too, Diana. What would have happened to Iggy if you hadn't found him and taken care of him? He might not have lived. One of the rarest creatures in the world might have died if not for you."

I felt self-conscious, listening to Lauren's compliment, so I looked at my feet. But then, feeling my throat tighten, I met her eyes, and nodded. I thought maybe Stephanie might have said a lot more, but she just smiled at us and said, "I'm proud of y'all."

"Thanks," I said. "I miss him. I loved his golden

eyes and that funny wise-crack smile he had. He was my little dragon for two days. I'll never forget him. I want to picture him bright blue and wandering free on Grand Cayman. Amazing to think that he could grow to be five feet long and live to be eighty years old!"

"Older than our Grammy!" Stephanie said.

And just at that moment, we saw our parents and Grammy and Luke coming up the stairs toward us. Grammy's new birthday necklace sparkled on her neck.

I thought, *Yes, she's my Grammy too. She made me feel like she was my very own grandmother.*

"There you are!" said Grammy. Her voice was like a song.

My new relatives surrounded us. The warmth of the sun embraced me, and a breath of wind caressed my cheek.

"Well," said Uncle Ted, "at the end of the day, I think we can say that this has been a fantastic trip!"

"Yeah!" we all said together.